Bearing Up Horseshoes

Bearing Up Horseshoes

Fiction By Jenny Pletcher Nolan

Jenny Nolan (signature)

ISBN: 978-0-557-50952-2

Contents

Acknowledgements:

Thanks to Mike, Jake, Julie, Gabrielle and Will. They each inspire me every day. I am blessed. This would not have happened without my husband's love and support.

Thank you to Patrice, Mimi and the entire Nolan clan for their encouragement. Thanks to Debby Mathias Burton for her excellent editing and kindness. Uyen Dugle, Lewis Anne Deputy, Jamie Abrams and Laura Hueni have been so very helpful and encouraging in their reading of the story throughout the process.

For the gang at the Indiana University Writer's Conference (June 2008), especially Karen Joy Fowler and Ross Gay, it was truly an amazing and extraordinary experience. Three books proved invaluable to my research of Johns and Kiawah Islands: A Place Called St. John's by Laylon W. Jordan and Elizabeth H. Stringfellow, Kiawah Island A History by Ashton Cobb, and Nature's Way on Kiawah by Bob Cowgill.

Three groups of women inspired me to write through their stories and their strength: The CRHP Team 4 of St. Vincent de Paul Church, The Benchmarks Committee (led by Megan Deputy Baughman) for the Women's Care Center of Elkhart, and The Thursday Club.

My brothers, Pete (Quake) and Matt Pletcher, are and always have been two of my very best friends. Quake pushed me and encouraged me throughout the writing of this story. Where would I be without them?

I must give a HUGE thank you to Dad and Nancy for introducing all of us to the beautiful little strip of the world that is Kiawah. The trips there with the Pletcher/Kidder/Nolan families are filled with moments to be treasured for a lifetime. Once again, we are all blessed by your leadership and love.

Lastly, my grandparents, Ike and Louise Pletcher, have forever served as an umbrella of peace and protection over my world. I thank them with all of my heart for always welcoming us into their sanctuary at Marl Lake. The Timm and Kay Pletcher and Steve and Linda Pletcher families have always been a special part of that place.

In loving memory: Lucille Hawkins, Hattie Line, Peggy DeSantis, Bill Nolan and Julie Ann Pletcher.

Chapter 1

T he dream was always the same.

It is a hot and humid summer night in northern Indiana. The mosquitoes are out in full force, and the brownish-red dirt from the ball diamonds blows across the dry pavement.

I'm watching Daddy's softball game. The sound of children chanting, "Hey batter, batter. Hey, batter!" rings in my ears along with the buzz of mosquitoes.

Why do I do this every time? I am foolishly standing alone at the end of the fence line. I'm sure I am outside of Momma's line of vision beneath the glaring overhead lights. I watch the moths dart around those lights, casting large flying shadows onto the pavement.

"Give him the riser, Bobby!" Daddy's friend, Mr. Frank, calls to the pitcher from his position in left field.

I hear him, but my face is turned to the west and south where dark storm clouds are gathering. It is dark, yet I can still see a yellow cast to the clouds. My stomach seems to flip-flop.

There she is. Out of the black cloud, she appears. She's not riding a broomstick, no poof of black smoke like in the movie. The Wicked Witch of the West is sitting atop a jet black carriage, whipping her equally jet-black horses into a frenzy.

She's coming across the railroad tracks to the south down Riverview Avenue. She screams at the horses to go faster, never letting up on the whip.

Her head is turned. She doesn't look at the horses or the direction the carriage takes. She's staring right at me.

I know Momma can't see me. Daddy's at shortstop, facing the opposite direction.

I want to run, but my feet seem to be frozen in place. I force myself closer to the rusty metal fence. My shoulder presses against the chain-link.

My palms are sweating. My heart beats fast in my chest. I feel like it might jump right out of my throat.

I would always wake up at that moment because she never came any closer.

I hadn't thought of that dream in a long time. Not until it took on a whole new life in the summer of 1979 while I was visiting Momma's family in South Carolina.

Chapter 2

M y back and neck are stiff from sleeping on the orange and brown shag carpeted floor of Daddy's conversion van. I have yet to open my eyes, but I am awake, wondering where we might be on our journey. Daddy, my brothers, and I are making our way down to the South Carolina coast. I can tell from the subtle turning of the van's wheels that we are most likely in the mountains of western North Carolina. This is a drive we have made often. This is the first time it has been made as a broken family.

Daddy likes to drive, and he likes to drive straight through the night while my brothers and I are sleeping. Less bickering that way is what Daddy says.

I can hear Daddy and Jay talking quietly in the front seats while Fret snores softly on the couch behind me. They are talking about the car Daddy's going to buy when he gets back home. I think he's decided on a brand new, deep blue 1979 Corvette with T-tops. Jay is very excited about the idea of Daddy owning a car like that. Jay will be fifteen soon which means driver's training and a learner's permit. Jay will be a ninth grader, and I will be a seventh grader at the same junior high school in the fall. I'll be thirteen in a few weeks.

"You awake, Em? We're heading down out of the mountains soon. I think we'll stop for breakfast near Spartanburg. There's bound to be a Waffle House there."

Daddy loves the Waffle House. That is his all-time favorite place to stop for a meal when we travel. Maybe he likes it because they're open twenty-four hours. Lord knows, the cooking cannot compare to my great grandmother Lydia's.

That is the reason for this long cross-country drive. Daddy's driving me and my brothers down to visit Momma's family for the month of July.

"The Waffle House sounds fine, Daddy."

He gives me a tired smile in the rearview mirror. Jay messes with the radio, looking for a station other than country.

I can't wait to get to the Low country to see Lydia. She has slowed down a bit. In her own words, she's no longer a spring chicken. I know she's still a strong and intimidating woman, and maybe some of that strength will rub off on me. Right now, I find myself, quite often, afraid.

Chapter 3

My great grandmother is a woman who boldly looks fear in the eye, and never has she lost the staring contest. She and Granddad live in a modest Low country style home out on River Road on Johns Island in the grand old state of South Carolina. Her home may be modest, but her rambling garden and her stature in the community are not.

Folks either love her or hate her, and the feeling is quite often mutual. Lydia doesn't mince words, and she cuts no slack. If you are true to your word and hard working, well then, you are the cat's meow . . . as good as hot butter biscuits, red-eye gravy and hominy grits on a Sunday morning. Lydia can read people like nobody's business. So if you have something to hide or like to put on airs, you might want to steer clear.

My brothers and I go down south and visit Lydia and the rest of Momma's family for at least a month each and every summer. I look forward to that month more than anything else all year long. We come down from northern Indiana into the lovely, steamy, stick-to-your-seat landscape of the Low country. Daddy thinks it's important for us to spend time with Lydia this summer in particular since our momma was killed in a car accident last spring.

Momma was Lydia's granddaughter, and she was raised by Lydia down on River Road. So, you see, not only do we need Lydia to feel a connection to Momma, but she needs us as well. She told me over the phone a couple weeks ago that after Momma was killed, she could have easily become a complete recluse drowning her sorrows in hard liquor and lemonade. Only through sheer willpower and the grace of God is she staying out of that slow-death trap. That's a path her own daughter has taken, but that's a whole other story.

As long as I can remember, I've felt the South coursing through my veins. It's like coming home each summer when Daddy pulls into the long drive at 44 River Road. The old house sits way back close to the river, just how close depends on the tides. It's a simple, white clapboard style with a gray tin roof, green shutters and an expanse of shady porch to the front and back which Lydia likes to call the veranda. Of course, it sits up at least eight feet off the ground in case of hurricane. All of River Road could lie six feet underwater in a particularly bad storm, at least that's what folks say. My brothers like to speculate a big storm brewing with each dark cloud passing overhead. They long to be caught up in an actual blow-your-shutters-off, palmetto-flattening hurricane. Or so they think.

Lydia's yard is planted with succulent fruits and vegetables, and the most gorgeous flowers, including my own favorite, hydrangeas. The hydrangeas are pale pink and vibrant blue, unlike the bland white ones back home. In fact, the entire Low country world seems to be in color, bright Technicolor, compared to the dull gray landscape up north. I feel like Dorothy leaving Kansas for Oz when I arrive. Yes, we have rivers back home and Lake Michigan, but the rivers do not change and live and move with the tide. We certainly don't have the Carolina beaches or the awe-inspiring Atlantic.

Lydia used to sell her flowers, fruits, and vegetables to many of Charleston's best restaurants, the restaurants attended by Charleston's social elite and the wealthy tourists to the area trying to put on southern airs . . . or maybe they just love it down here as much as I do. The course of time has slowed Lydia down a bit, but she still keeps a mighty fine garden. The scale is just not as grand as it once was.

Speaking real quick in regards to "wealthy tourists," my great grandmother always says that it's not the kind of purse a woman carries or the jewelry she wears but what she has in the bank, in land ownership, and, most importantly, in "God's work" that define wealth. She tells us not to judge by appearances because folks out to impress humankind most often do not impress the good Lord.

She reminds us often that "charity begins at home." My brothers and I are constantly trying to figure out what exactly she means by many of her "old saws," but that one's clear. First, you need to take care of your family.

This old River Road home has been in Lydia's family since just after the Civil War. Believe it or not, Lydia's grandfather, Frederic Ridenour, was a Union soldier who just flat-out fell in love with the Low country. He stumbled upon this land trying to get back north after the surrender by the Confederates and General Robert E. Lee.

The home and much of River Road had been part of a Charleston family's plantation, but not quite as you might envision a plantation to be. Many northern folks have romantic visions of grandeur in regards to southern plantation homes, but really this was just a simple Low country working farm situated on the river to catch a cool breeze in the summer if at all possible . . . a place to escape that stifling, stale heat of Charleston.

My little brother, Fret (he's nine,) hates to go to Charleston on an especially hot day even today because he gags and retches at the stench of those touristy horse and carriage rides. Fret likes to comment on the fact that cars were invented for a reason, and he doesn't understand why horses must still trot along the streets of Charleston, polluting the already heavy air.

Anyway, Lydia's Grandfather Ridenour purchased this old, abandoned plantation home and then went north to fetch his bride. He got an awfully good price for it, but most folks weren't too sure about a Yankee moving into these parts. The wounds from the war were too fresh, but Grandfather Ridenour and his sweet bride, Cecille, were quick to make friends. Grandmother Cecille was French-born, so not only were folks drawn to her foreign ways and thick accent but that lady could cook southern-style with the best of them. By the time my great grandmother, Lydia, came along, the family was practically born-and-raised Southern.

Granddad is Lydia's second husband and is as sweet as a summer day is long, sweeter even than Lydia's delicious pecan pie. Granddad thinks Lydia just hangs the moon, and she feels the same way about him. She can be feisty and impatient with him, but he knows her aim is true. He also enjoys her spirited nature and often winks at us and chuckles when she's in the middle of a rant. Lydia then turns and gives all of us her "Go to heck" eyebrow. That's what she calls it when she raises one eyebrow way up high and drops the other down low over her eye. This look involves not a single word to let us know exactly what she is feeling. I often practice my own "Go to heck" eyebrow in the bathroom mirror.

Chapter 4

I open my eyes with a start and wonder where on earth I am.

I am in her room, the room where she slept when she was my age.

At home, since Momma died, I would hesitate to awaken, wanting to hang on to the dream-filled memories of her life with me.

But this dream was terrible. She was here with me in the Low country as she has been in other summers. We were sitting under the oak together out by the river. She was laughing and telling me stories from her own childhood spent on the river. She suddenly became serious and quiet. Tears formed in the corners of her soft brown eyes.

It was here, Sugar, in this place I treasure more than any other.

This is where it happened.

I try to ask her what happened but the wind is blowing, and she doesn't seem to hear my question.

How could I have let that happen? My whole world was shattered on that day.

The wind is blowing even harder. I try to console her, to ask her what is wrong. Why was her world shattered, but she doesn't hear me. She can't even see me any more.

As if I'm nothing more than a rag doll, the wind blows me over backwards. As I go, I see Momma tumbling in the opposite direction. When I force myself up on my knees and look for her, she is gone. The river water seems to ripple in a circle at the edge.

Chapter 5

I started jogging with Momma a couple summers ago, and we had matching Nikes. That was the first I'd ever heard of Nike, and distance running was just becoming popular. Momma had a little weight to lose, not too much, but she started jogging for that reason. I went out with her one day out of boredom and found out I was kind of good at it. Since then, I've been in a little AAU track club back home, running the 880 and the mile. The ribbons I've won now adorn my big red scrapbook that I keep on a bookshelf in my room in Indiana.

Momma got a horrible sunburn at one of my track meets a week before she was killed, and for some reason, that's all I can picture now when I see her in my mind's eye. She wore a deep V-neck t-shirt that day, and I remember her showing me that V-shaped sunburn on her chest. We giggled about it at the time. There was not a viewing at her funeral because of the horrific toll the car accident had on her beautiful face, but somehow I see that V-shaped sunburn as she lies in the casket.

I pull on my shorts and Jay's IU t-shirt and quietly pad my way down the long mahogany-floored hallway and stairs. I follow the aroma of strong, freshly percolated coffee to the kitchen. Of course, Lydia is up with the sun.

"Good morning, Sug," she croons in her raspy, yet completely feminine voice.

Sug is short for Sugar, and I love the nickname.

"It is divine having y'all here. I've been looking forward to your visit for what seems an eternity."

"I've been counting down the days since school let out. I'm going out for a run. Will you save me a cup of coffee?"

Lydia pulls me into an embrace and kisses the top of my head. I can faintly smell cigarette smoke and Chanel No. Five perfume mingling with the coffee.

"As long as you don't mind it strong enough to bear up a horseshoe!"

We laugh together. Once again, I'm not sure what that old saw means exactly, but I know the coffee is strong. Anything less strong is dubbed "panther piss" by Lydia. As long as there's plenty of milk and sugar, I wouldn't drink it any other way.

She gives me another quick hug and a cool thermos of lemonade to take out with me.

I take a couple sips as I step out onto the side veranda from the kitchen. It is already a steamy morning. I sit on a rocker on the veranda to double knot my Nikes, set the lemonade under the rocker and take in the view from the back of the house. The garden stretches before me almost to River Road, and I can see Kona, Lydia's Border collie, sniffing around after something in the hydrangeas.

"Come here, Kona." I quietly call and she comes bounding up the steps to greet me. "Hello, baby, how are you this morning? Were you after something in the bushes?" Kona rolls over on her back so that I can pat her tummy. I give her a kiss on the head and trot down the back steps. The dog watches me from the porch with a look of pure contentment. Granddad takes Kona for a long walk each morning before he goes off to work, so I imagine that is the reason for her porch-dwelling satisfaction.

It's probably a quarter mile up Lydia and Granddad's drive, so I walk the distance to warm up my legs, stopping occasionally to stretch. When I reach River Road, I decide to run to the north towards the intracoastal bridge and Charleston. It's about two miles to the bridge, so to cross it and come back is a nice four and a half to five mile run. Sometimes I go in the other direction, which is a flatter run, in the direction of my beloved Kiawah Island.

I start at an easy pace waiting for my body to warm to the rhythm of the run. My joints can ache a bit to start, but as my muscles warm, the run becomes peaceful and freeing. I try to time my breathing, two breaths in through my nose and one longer breath out to the beat of my steps. Since Momma's been gone, my jogging has become running.

Sometimes I feel like I am running away from the urge to rip and tear and scream.

I feel bad sometimes because I can get angry with my brothers or Daddy, but maybe boys are different, better at keeping their feelings to themselves. That is why I'm so happy to be here. Lydia and I have always shared some sort of special bond.

I replay what I can remember of my dream in my head, wondering how I could have kept Momma with me a bit longer.

I realize any aching is gone and the run is feeling good. The road is bordered by live oaks covered in Spanish moss. I imagine them hiding an escaped slave or clandestine lovers. I like that word for secret, clandestine.

I'd never paid particularly close attention to this before, but now I notice a cross and old fake flowers, faded by the elements, nailed to one amazingly large old live oak standing dangerously close to the road. I wonder about the person who died there and the family left behind. Do they talk about their loss and the painful void left in place of the deceased, or do they go on as if nothing ever happened? As if that person never even existed.

My breathing comes heavier as I start to climb the Freedman Memorial Bridge. I recall my track coach, Mr. Gove, telling us to climb on our toes, not flat-footed. He tells us to take the hill, don't let it take you. I increase my pace, breathing hard. My calves and hamstrings seem to be fighting one another for pain dominance. My shins hurt, but I keep going.

I can feel the sun shining hot upon the right side of my face. I look to my left to see the crabbers out in full force along the shallow creek beds of the tidal marsh. My stomach grumbles as I imagine a delicious lunch of savory crab cakes or sweet and spicy she-crab soup, dishes for which this region is famous. I know Fret would love to be down there chasing those crabs, but he would then gag at the thought of eating them. Fret might eat an occasional crab cake, but he does not want to get to know the crab on a personal level before he eats it! Jay, on the other hand, has no problem catching his dinner. In pioneer days, it would have been easy for him to survive.

It is low tide, so I can see the blue crabs scampering along the muddy creek banks. The salted, swamp-gas smell of the balmy air swirls around me as I climb the bridge. I happen to love that smell. The snowy egrets, and an occasional pelican or heron fly low over the shallow water searching for breakfast.

A scene like this is a gentle reminder of God's love for us, I believe, maybe even a sweet reminder of Momma's love for me. Just as some people are placed in our lives to guide us in the right paths, maybe scenes and situations provide those same opportunities. Too many people, grown people even, go through life never noticing though. Lydia says that it is much easier for children to notice the gifts we are given in the everyday randomness of life than for adults. She says you can hear recognition in children's laughter and see it in their tears.

As I reach the top of the bridge, I decide to turn around and head back home instead of crossing down to the other side. Running to the other side means I have to climb back up, and, suddenly, I don't feel like one more uphill run.

Chapter 6

I t is still early as I slow to a walk and turn up the lane. Some sort of old, light blue convertible passes by on River Road. The driver honks as he passes the lane, and I can see fishing poles hanging out of the back seat. It looks like a couple teenage boys in front, laughing and waving. I have no idea who they are but wave anyway.

My clothes drip with sweat from the run and the heavy heat of a South Carolina summer morning. Kona does not notice me as I approach the back garden area. The dog is too busy rustling among the wildflower beds. "Kona, you'd better get out of there quick before Lydia catches you in her flowers!"

The beautiful, long-haired, black dog hears my voice and finds what she's digging for at the same time. She comes loping out of the garden with a faded green tennis ball held between her teeth. "Alright, baby, let's play catch."

I toss the ball high into the air in the direction of the house, and Kona runs at full speed, makes a perfect leap into the air and catches the ball squarely in her mouth.

Laughter from the front veranda draws my attention to the bike parked near the back steps. I recognize the pink frame, big fuzzy seat cushion and straw basket with fake daisies adorning it immediately as belonging to Lydia's closest neighbor to the north, Ms. Claudette Jenkins. Lydia often says the woman was born to be on stage because drama follows her wherever she goes.

I know why she's here. Ms. Claudette has come to pay her "respects" to Daddy before he heads back to Indiana today. I can feel my pulse quickening and the anger rising inside my belly as I make my way around to the front or river side of the house.

Fortunately, Ms. Claudette has her back to my approach, and Lydia catches my anxious glare first. She gives me a big smile and a double eyebrow raise while motioning for me to sit next to her. Her visitor sees Lydia gesture and turns.

"Oh, you poor darling dear, Emmy, what are you doing out running on a steamy morning like this? Yer around all them boys entirely too much! Lydia, we gots to teach this little gal the ways of a young lady this summer. Specially now with her momma being gone and all."

I ignore Ms. Claudette's reference to my deceased mother. "Why, good morning to you too, Ms. Jenkins."

"Claudette, Em, call me Claudette."

"You are sure up early paying a visit, Ms. Claudette. I recognized your pretty pink bike out back and heard your laughter lighting up the heavy morning air. I had to come around front to see what was so darn comical." I smile warmly at Ms. Claudette then glance nervously in Daddy's direction. Daddy does not tolerate insolent behavior. Rude children are not his cup of tea, if you get my drift.

Daddy says I can get carried away with language when speaking to adults. You see, in the fourth grade, my teacher, Mrs. Agniel, told Momma I had a gift for Language Arts. Well, Momma took Mrs. Agniel's advice and encouraged my reading of poetry, literature, and even the dictionary. I remember reading Frances Hodgson Burnett's The Secret Garden with a dictionary by my side. Sometimes the dictionary didn't even help with the way some of those country characters spoke. That same school year, Momma and Daddy became tired of my gift for Language Arts and strongly encouraged me to give up sarcasm for Lent.

Lydia recognizes the sarcasm in my voice as I speak to Ms. Claudette. The real mystery is why Daddy sits over there smiling while watching this scene unfold before him.

"C'mon, Sug, and sit here by me. Ms. Jenkins just wanted to come by and say hello to your daddy before he heads back home. It was awfully nice of you to come by, Claudette."

Lydia says this as way of dismissal, but Ms. Claudette doesn't take the hint. She is dressed in a tennis outfit to suit her individual sense of style. To me, the outfit looks like something Petunia Pig might wear in a really bad children's ballet recital. As she stands, I catch a glimpse of lacy bloomers beneath her flouncy tennis skirt.

Daddy is sitting on the porch swing. His dark hair seems longer than usual. It hangs down over his eyebrows, and he looks exhausted. Ms. Claudette sits beside him and places her bejeweled hand on his arm.

"Jack, your Meredith was my very closest little friend coming up." With this false statement, Ms. Jenkins begins sobbing uncontrollably. "Of course we traveled in different social circles. I was such a snob, but I loved that girl." She dramatically pulls a handkerchief from her ample bosom while leaning in closer to Daddy.

Lydia puts a gentle hand on my arm.

"If you ever need anything, anything at all," Ms. Claudette says. She's practically purring in Daddy's direction, "You just call on Ms. Claudette."

Daddy coughs. "Why, thank you for your kind words, Claudette. I appreciate you dropping by this morning."

This time she picks up the cue to exit.

"I best be drying my eyes and getting on to my morning tennis match. We have a mighty fine new pro out at Kiawah, and, y'all, I don't just mean his tennis game. Ooowee, that young man could make me forget I'm a Christian woman. Give my love to those boys of yours, Jack, and Emmy, I'd love to have you over for tea one afternoon. Perhaps I can teach you the art of enjoying a fine cup of English tea." Ms. Jenkins says this distractedly while smoothing her tennis skirt over her upper thighs and disappearing around the corner of the house.

Lydia and I watch Daddy watch her retreat.

"Yes, ma'am," I call and when she's gone, "over my dead body."

Chapter 7

W e hear laughter sounding from the bushes down by the riverbank, and Jay and Fret come running up the slight slope with Kona on their heels.

"Man!" Fret yells. Fret is nine years old and a pure ball of energy. "I thought Ms. Jenkins was never going to leave. I'm starving, but I was afraid that woman might smother me like she tried to do to Daddy."

Jay quietly chases our little brother on to the veranda. He is smiling, and that's not something I've seen him do too much of lately. If he would just let himself have a good cry, he might start to heal a bit. Unfortunately, he has followed Daddy's lead and decided to simply ignore the whole situation.

Maybe July will bring Jay some healing. He loves the Low country as much as I do. He enjoys fishing in the river, late night crabbing on the beach with Uncle Ty and long bike rides along this peaceful and gorgeous terrain.

"Hop off the bus, Gus. Don't need to discuss much. Just drop off the key, Lee, and get yourself free!" Fret is hopping around the veranda now putting on a show with Lydia's urging. Daddy is laughing at his little boy's dance moves, and even Jay is singing along.

"How about some biscuits and gravy?" Lydia says then. "Granddad picked the last of the strawberries before he left too."

The boys follow Lydia into the kitchen.

Daddy calls me over to the porch swing. I sit down next to him and cuddle right into the crook of his arm as he drapes it around my shoulders.

"I'm going to miss you over the next three weeks, Em. You guys get along for me while you're here, okay?" Daddy pulls me closer and starts to say something else, but stops himself.

"We'll get along just fine, Daddy," I promise. "And, I'm gonna miss you too. Daddy . . ." I hesitate.

"Yes, Sugar." He uses the name Lydia and Momma always use, and it makes me cry.

"Daddy, please be careful driving home. And call right when you get there, okay?"

He wipes his own eyes. "I will, Sug. I will."

Chapter 8

My body is a perfect upside-down cannonball in the air before I extend pencil-straight legs and pointed toes toward the sky, reaching my arms over my head for the sweet river water. I know the water is sweet because I cannot keep from smiling beneath it and laugh out loud as I reach the surface. That is how happy this cool water and hot, cloudless Carolina day make me feel.

My brothers, Jay and Fret, have joined me in the river now, and I can hear their shrieks as I turn my face to the sun and float on my back. Uncle Ty, Momma's brother, is captain of the pontoon boat. He turns up the Beach Boys song *Be True to Your School* while Aunt Katy and our cousin, Ben, dance on the deck.

Uncle Ty is the biggest Beach Boys and Elvis fan I know. He would have traveled the entire state of South Carolina to hear either of them play live. He has even been known to show up at a party impersonating Elvis - bejeweled jumpsuit, wig, and all. We have a real love of music as a family. Daddy tends to like rock music, such as Jerry Lee Lewis, Buddy Holly, or The Rolling Stones. Momma was a fan of Simon and Garfunkel, Charlie Pride, and Roberta Flack, not to mention Stevie Wonder. Momma had a beautiful voice. I enjoyed riding on errands in the car with her just so I could hear her sing along with the radio.

Lydia and Granddad listen to old big band or "Brat-Pack" music, as Lydia likes to call it, but she also loves church hymns and "old negro spirituals." She often says that the black folk of these islands have really got it right when they worship. She says God gives us these emotions, and we should certainly not be afraid to use the complete array when worshipping the good Lord. I agree with her. That's why I love to attend Holy Spirit Catholic Church when I'm here in the Low country.

Holy Spirit is not at all like our lily-white Catholic Church back home. Folks with all varying shades of skin color attend this church and, as the name implies, the Holy Spirit is truly present there. My best friend down here, Abby, her momma is the choir director. Abby sings with the choir. That girl has the voice of an angel. Abby's momma, Mrs. Janie Doyle, let's me sing with them when I am visiting. Mrs. Doyle plays the piano (not a tired, old organ) like nobody's business, and the entire congregation is moved to sing along.

One Christmas back home, our choral director tried to lead the congregation in a rousing, toe-tapping rendition of *Go Tell it on the Mountain*. There was a tambourine, hand-clapping, and all but believe me when I say some folks really do not feel the Lord's love in a musical beat. I'll bring up another of Lydia's old saws here, "If we all liked the same thing, we'd all still be driving black Fords. To each his own."

I am floating along on my back, thinking all these musical thoughts when I feel a tug on my leg.

"Gotcha, Em!" Fret yells, "You daydream more than anyone I have ever seen."

He swims away and, of course, I must chase after him now. Jay is holding Ben's hand and jumping off the front of the pontoon boat as we approach.

"Emmy, did you see me? I'm a dolphin!" Ben yells this in the adorable way that only a three year old can. It's like a kiss from God on one's soul.

Jay proceeds to toss Ben in the air towards me and Fret. Fret dives under Ben as I catch him. "You are the most handsome dolphin I have ever seen, Ben." The day, the water, the music filling the summer air, there is joy and healing in this river.

I take turns with my brothers diving around our cousin, causing him to burst into laughter over and over with each squirt of water from our mouths. He bobs in his yellow lifejacket, squirming every which way to avoid the streams of water. I glance up to the boat to see Aunt Katy and Uncle Ty snuggled together. They are smiling, but not smiling. I wonder if they are missing my momma or just feeling a little heartsick watching the three motherless children playing with their boy.

A far-off whistle pierces the air and carries over the water. The sun is beginning to drop in the sky, and Lydia is giving us the signal that her picnic dinner is about to be served on the pier. Aunt Katy waits on the boat with her arms full of soft, colorful beach towels. Jay swims Ben back while Fret and I wait our turns.

"Uncle Ty, can the three of us swim back to the pier?" asks Jay.

"If you carry jackets with you, or y'all can take this raft . . ." Uncle Ty hands Jay an inflated raft long enough for all of us to hold onto and kick.

"Me too?" yells Ben.

"You too?" Aunt Katy laughs. "You are trying to grow up way too fast, little boy."

"I'm not little. I'm a big guy."

"Yes, a big guy who is going to stay on this boat with his momma right now." Aunt Katy wraps Ben in a warm towel and pulls him close. He stops protesting.

Chapter 9

I am in the middle with a brother on each side and feel quite happy to have the raft. I am ready to have some help staying above water right now.

Ben and Aunt Katy wave from the pontoon boat as it glides by.

The tide is coming in, and we float along wordlessly as the waves of the swelling river lap around us. Laughter carries across the water as Uncle Ty and Aunt Katy reach the pier. We hear Lydia and Granddad fighting over who gets to grab Ben off the boat. We hear Kona barking.

"Yo ho, Yo ho, a pirate's life for me!" Fret starts the old pirate sea chantey quietly as we slowly kick along. None of us seems to be in any particular hurry.

"Yo ho, Yo ho, a pirate's life for me!" I sing along.

"Da, da, da, da-da, da, da, dee, da, da-da, da, daaa! Yo ho, Yo ho, a pirate's life for me." We don't know the actual verses of the song, and they are probably entirely inappropriate for young mouths (and ears) anyway.

Fret is completely fascinated with pirates right now. "Remember, Em, on the *Pirates of the Caribbean* ride how you screamed thinking that cannonball was about to hit our boat! I thought you were going to fall out the other side trying to get away . . ."

"Oh, Fret, you weren't too brave when the boat suddenly went over that waterfall," says Jay.

"Remember the lady chasing the pirate with her broom?" I ask.

"Remember the pirate sitting right above us with his hairy leg and nasty foot hanging down?" Jay asks.

"Remember how bad the foot smelled?" Fret says.

"Now that is carrying the whole thing too far," I say while smiling at my little brother. "You don't remember that."

"We're lucky to have had that trip together before Momma . . ." Jay stops talking.

I try to think of us as lucky.

* * *

We have arrived at the pier. As we lift ourselves up carefully avoiding the sharp oyster shells stuck to the ladder, Lydia says quietly, "Look at the dolphins."

I can smell Lydia's fried chicken and macaroni and cheese, and a hunger pang hits me hard right in the gut. However, I turn to see my favorite sight of the Low country. It's as if the dolphins were following us to Lydia's pier. As if their graceful water ballet is just for us. Even little Ben watches. There are four or five of them and they are obviously catching their dinner. Their gray noses break the surface to dive back face first in that ever-lovely dolphin arch. I wonder if they are friends. I wonder if they are family.

The sun drops behind Lydia and Granddad's house. The Carolina night air is still quite warm and humid, but my brothers and I huddle into the warm towels together on the pontoon boat. Uncle Ty and Granddad light torches at the end of the pier while Lydia and Aunt Katy pass around ice cold bottles of Coca-Cola to the kids. Ben sits on my lap, relaxing comfortably in his St. Louis Cardinal pajamas.

While Lydia fixes our plates, we talk about the day and the dolphins. We wonder where Daddy might be on his trip home. Lydia hands me a plate of perfectly fried chicken and thick, rich homemade mac and cheese, crispy on top. On the side, there's a cool salad of fresh-picked cucumber, tomato, and onions tossed with a bit of salt, pepper, oil, vinegar and, of course, just a touch of "sug."

As we prepare to eat, Lydia asks us to bow our heads in thanks. I bow my head while taking a peek around at our family gathered here in the torchlight. Granddad stands tall next to Lydia. I can see how he probably was a very handsome man in his day. Lydia will say, jokingly, that when she married him he looked like a Greek god, and now he looks like a gosh darn Greek. Then she says "pardon my French" because she actually uses the swear words in place of my gosh darn, if you know what I mean. Jay is on the other side of Granddad with his dark head of hair already bowed in prayer, Fret is on Jay's other side, flashing me his toothless, nine-year-old smile, followed by Uncle Ty, Aunt Katy holding Ben, and back to Lydia to complete the circle.

Chapter 10

U ncle Ty and Aunt Katy have taken Ben and gone home.
Granddad sits on the settee on the veranda drinking a cold Pabst
Blue Ribbon and smoking a cigarette. I have just returned from helping
Lydia carry the last of the dishes into the kitchen. Jay has extinguished
the torches at the end of the pier and sits down on the porch swing,
away from the smoke of Granddad's cigarette.

"It's the last of our vices," Lydia says as she lights her own
cigarette.

"It's really bad for you," Jay states quietly.

"Old habits die hard, dear. Don't ever start."

Kona barks at Fret down by the riverbank as he comes jumping out
of the large live oak. He calls to us from the spot in the yard where he's
landed. "Lydia, will you tell us the story of Angel Oak?"

"Again, Frettie? That's the first story you want to hear each time
you come for a visit. You want me to do the telling or Granddad?"

"You go right ahead, darling. I'll be turning in here shortly."

"You kids alright with hearing the old tale again?"

"Yes, ma'am," says Jay.

I nod my head.

"Okay then get on up here and have a seat, Fret! Well, now, there
are stories in abundance down here relating to love and the trees. But
Angel Oak is the story of forbidden love."

Fret sits next to Jay and nods his head in agreement. Jay listens
with his eyes closed, and I feel immediately as if I've entered a dream.
I can already picture the large tree located up Marlcreek Highway in
my head.

"Miss Lily, a young plantation gal, fell in love with the handsome and assertive overseer named Jim Lee. Miss Lily's father was an extremely powerful man around here at that point in time. His name was Master Raymond Bennington, and Master Bennington strongly opposed any interaction between the two. He made it clear to his overseer that he would be out of a job, if he went anywhere near Miss Lily Bennington. He also informed Miss Lily that the convent would be very happy to receive first his money and then his daughter. Master Bennington believed a heavy hand would keep the two apart. Often this is the mistake of men who are used to getting their way in business.

"Needless to say, the couple quietly met, night after night up in the branches of that Oak, expressing love for one another through shy, yet passionate, kisses and conversations outlining dreams for a future that was not meant to be. On one of those nights, the couple decided to meet the next night at the stroke of midnight with bags packed for an elopement. They mistakenly believed Master Bennington couldn't possibly turn them away when they returned as a married couple.

"Well, Miss Lily confided in her constant companion and nursemaid, Nell, who felt obligated to tell Miss Lily's momma, the Mrs. Bennington, the whole plan. Speaking in defense of Mrs. Bennington, she did not yet know that her husband was a stark raving mad lunatic. So, she told him the entire plot, thinking she could somehow preserve the family's good standing in the parish.

"Miss Lily met her lover, her affianced, as planned beneath that oak, but Miss Lily's daddy was watching from the shadows. He leapt out as the paramours embraced, and promptly sent Miss Lily to her bedchamber. As Miss Lily left weeping, she heard Jim Lee begging her father for Miss Lily's hand in marriage. Bennington would hear none of it. He told the young man that he was not good enough to wipe the dirt from his daughter's silk slippers and that all he would ever be is a dead-end cracker in a dead-end cracker job.

"Miss Lily reached her room with a view of the oak, the tree she once climbed up into on a daily basis to inspect the world around her. She grew into a woman in the branches of that tree. Miss Lily sat on her high bed with a fluffy pillow in her lap. She reminisced, mentally blocking the sounds of the argument outside.

"Sitting upon a sturdy branch and leaning back to gaze upward into the tree was a favorite pastime. Often butterflies and bees would flit and buzz about over her head, occasionally alighting on her own limbs. She would watch birds mate and nest in the spring. She would watch the progression of their hatchlings as they grew into fully free flying creatures themselves.

"Oh, how Miss Lily longed to fly from the old branches of that oak, even as a very young child.

"A single gunshot awakened Miss Lilly from her reverie. She hurried to the window in time to see her once-beloved daddy standing over her dead beau, gun still smoking.

"A few days of anguish and sorrow later (on Miss Lily and her mother, oh, and Nell's part) Master Bennington left the house on his usual grounds tour. After all, he did have to look into the hiring of a new (preferably homely) overseer on that day.

"Master Bennington noticed a beautiful bare foot dangling from within the oak. He called out to Miss Lily, hoping perhaps that would be the day she forgave him and moved on with her life. His thought was that the girl needed to come to her senses because her father was only protecting her from that overly-aggressive, uppity cracker.

"But there would be no forgiveness on that day for Master Bennington. Only lifeless eyes stared back at him from within the tree, but those eyes were still asking 'why?' It looked as if Miss Lily climbed right up into that tree and died of pure heartache. It was always rumored the tears were not even dry on her face when her daddy found her.

"Ever since that day, the old tree has been called Angel Oak. Folks will still see, on occasion, the young lovers embracing beneath it on an especially foggy night. Some folks have even seen Master Bennington on his knees, weeping beneath that tree. I don't know of anyone who's been brave enough to climb up into her branches. It is said that Miss Lily can be heard singing way up high, and she might just squeeze the life out of anyone who ventures on up to hear her."

"Can someone really die of pure heartache?" Fret has positioned his long-legged child's body on Lydia's lap during the course of the story.

"I often wonder about that myself, darling. However, if that is the case, I figure the good Lord would have taken me long ago." Lydia stares down past the tree into the depths of the river.

Chapter 11

I hand the phone off to Jay in the front hallway and head toward the kitchen, Lydia, and the smell of strong coffee. I smelled the coffee as soon as I heard the phone ringing.

"Good morning, Sug. How's your daddy doing?" Lydia reaches into the cupboard for a coffee cup.

"Daddy's fine. He's talking to Jay now. He's playing golf this morning." I exhale loudly.

Lydia looks at me. The woman is amazing. She doesn't even enter the kitchen until she has dressed and swept her long light red hair up into a French twist. The eyebrow is up.

"Why does he have to go play golf on a Sunday morning? Why can't he be like my friend's daddies and go to church?"

"Oh, Sugar, hasn't your daddy been there for you? He's not out drinking, running around, and neglecting his duties as a father, is he?"

I stare at Lydia.

"I said, is he?"

"No, ma'am." I reply with my head hanging low, feeling as if I have a tail between my legs like a mangy old dog.

"Then, Emma Cecille, it is not our place to judge. Your daddy is doing all he can for you kids, besides each person comes to the Lord in his own time. No one is perfect, Sug, and the sooner you come to accept that fact in this old world, the better off you will be. Jesus set us the perfect example, and all of our lives we might try to live up to that. But to think we might ever attain it is a sad mistake. That's just the problem with some of these 'holier than thou' folks. They stop growing in their faith because they think they're already there. Instead of looking at ways to improve their own lives, they sit in judgment of everyone else. 'Christian' is not a title so much as it is a life-long process. In the end, we can only hope and pray that our lives have evolved in a way that is pleasing to the Lord.

"Remember, Sug. Your daddy is all alone raising you kids now, and maybe he needs time on the golf course as a release from his duties as a businessman and a father. God is present on the golf course if your daddy wants Him to be. Knowing you, I'll bet you met with Him on your run yesterday morning."

Lydia embraces me as she finishes her defense of Daddy.

I know that she has grown in her faith later in life and can truly understand Daddy. She will support him because charity begins at home.

"Lydia, I know all of that is most likely true. I know Daddy's a good person. It's confusing though when I hear at mass that a person must accept Jesus as Lord and savior to enter into the kingdom of heaven. The priests say that all the time."

"Just a mustard seed, Sug. That is what the good book says."

Chapter 12

I am walking out of Holy Spirit Catholic Church arm-in-arm with my very best Low country friend, Miss Abby Doyle. Abby is short like me and dark-haired, but that is where our likenesses cease. I am quick to tan in the summer, and she is white as a bed sheet even living down here year-round! My eyes are brown, and hers are deep blue, almost violet, really. Her momma says they are a perfect match for Elizabeth Taylor's. We are, however, both quick with a laugh and a smile. That is probably what makes us best of friends. Oh, there is an extreme difference in that Abby loves Donny Osmond, to the point of regularly wearing purple socks! She also loves Barry Manilow and claims to be related to Elvis on her mother's side. I find it hard to believe, but it would explain their musical talent.

The only song I really like by Barry Manilow is *Mandy*, and that's only because I once had a Great Dane puppy named Mandy. Momma and Daddy thought she was getting too big for our home and yard. Plus, she regularly dragged me around the block, ripping my clothes when I tried to walk her. My parents sent her away to live on a farm. It ties in perfectly with the song to the point that whenever I hear it, I cry.

Another thing Abby and I have in common . . . both of our youngest siblings are adopted. Betsy, her baby sister, is a little blond pale thing, whereas Fret has black, curly hair and skin the color of coffee with cream.

I don't know why the Doyle family adopted Betsy, but I know in our case Momma had a very difficult time giving birth to me and Jay. She and Daddy wanted more children, so they went to Catholic Services for help. They were told it might take years to adopt a white baby. Momma squeezed Daddy's hand and told the lady they could love and provide for any child, no matter the color. I know she squeezed Daddy's hand at that moment because I used to beg her to tell me that story about how my little brother came to be ours.

I can't imagine my life without Fret. Don't get me wrong, we can fight like a couple of alley cats. Do not call him my *adopted* brother unless you'd like a fist-fight on your hands. He's my brother just as Jay is. Nothing can change that, and I know Jay feels the same way.

His name is actually Frederic after Lydia's Grandfather Ridenour, but the little guy used to cling to Momma as a toddler. He never wanted her out of his sight, so Jay started calling him Fret, always worrying. Jay loves to come up with nick names, and Fret's stuck.

"Look over there, Emmy. That's the new family that moved to the island last fall, the Feegans. They live out on Kiawah, but the youngest boy, Blake, attends Johns Middle with us."

"The tall blond boy? He's just as cute as you told me in your letters."

"He's just as nice as he is cute too. Now that's really saying something since most boys in my class are as rude as can be!"

Abby sees Blake looking over our way. She smiles and waves. Blake waves back, but he seems to look at me in an odd way. He is a broad-shouldered boy with white blond hair and a tanned, yet fair complexion. He's a bit of a distance away, but I can tell his eyes are practically turquoise even from here. He waves again and turns to follow his family piling into an old blue convertible.

Abby is a bit boy-crazy. I'm not. I stop watching him when I realize Abby is speaking to me.

"There's no use staring after him like that, Em. He is way too busy with school, sports, and his huge family to have time for girls."

I have a feeling she must have gotten a bit of the cold shoulder from the boy herself.

"I wasn't staring, Miss Abigail Doyle. I was thinking . . ."

Lydia walks over to us looking elegant, as usual, in her red wedge mules with equally red toenails peeking through, black gauchos, and red and black floral pattern short-sleeved blouse. Her sunglasses are large, tortoise-shell in the style of her all time favorite first lady, Jackie Kennedy.

"Let's go, gals. I told Marcy we'd be out right after mass."

Chapter 13

M s. Marcy's café, Gracenote, is out at the Ladyfish Marina. Marcy was Momma's best friend growing up. They did just about everything together and saw one another through a great many hard times, but even more good times. They were practically inseparable until they went away to college.

Marcy stayed in Charleston to study the culinary arts. She and her husband, Curtis Hann, grew up together, but began dating in college. He studied marine biology at Clemson, and now teaches at Johns High. He is also part of the Natural Preservation Plan Committee for Kiawah Island.

Momma decided upon high school graduation to spread her wings and fly this Low country coop. She went north to Indiana University in Bloomington, Indiana to study nursing, and that is where she met Daddy. As much as Momma loved the Low country, she hated it too. Everyone down here knew her family history regarding her own mother, and she was tired of the gossip. Normally decent folks can turn mighty ugly when it comes to a juicy bit of gossip, and Momma's mother, my Grandma Rae, provided folks with plenty opportunity to gossip.

Momma and Daddy fell in love in their sophomore year of college, got married, moved into married housing, and had my brother, Jay. They were poor as church mice supporting one another, a baby, and two educations, but they made it.

Marcy came up north right away when she heard about Momma's accident. She sat with us in our den, searching for the right words, but not much was said. I wanted to wrap my arms around her and tell her we'd all be okay, but I wasn't sure. It's odd to be twelve years old watching adults drowning in anguish all around you. I've learned to pretty much keep my sorrow to myself. Not that adults don't want to know my pain, but they can't help.

Now I am hanging on as if my life depended on it. Tears are flowing like the River Nile. Marcy pushes me gently away and stares into my eyes. Not with pity but understanding. She knows these tears bring fertile life and hope to this barren desert.

Marcy wipes the tears from her own eyes. "Oh, Sug, I am thrilled beyond measure to see you. You've grown since last I saw ya, girl, and you're looking more like your sweet momma everyday."

"Thanks, Miss Marcy, but I'll never be as pretty as she was." I mean it.

"Modesty is a fine virtue, my dear Emmy. So how about some sweet tea? Abby, Lydia, sweet tea?"

Lydia follows Marcy inside with an offer to help.

Abby and I walk to the edge of the dock and sit with our feet dangling toward the river water. We both have our church-going sandals strapped on tight. We stare for a moment at the tiny mud crabs scampering on the rocks below. Abby punches my shoulder gently and points farther down the bank where a dead stingray has washed up on the rocks.

"Well, Em, lunch smells a lot better than this here riverbank. I'm so glad you're here . . . summer has been boooor-ing."

"I was bored at home. We did start cheer practice. That's been fun, I guess. I did make a couple new friends on the squad. That's it for excitement in Indiana."

"Speaking of cheerleaders . . . you will never guess who our sponsor is!"

"Uh, Ms. Hat?"

We both laugh at the thought of Miss Marcy's mother-in-law being the cheer sponsor.

"I have no idea, Abby. Who is it?"

"Ms. Jenkins. Ms. Claudette Jenkins. Can you believe it? She's trying to teach us all the manners of a fine Southern woman. I feel like shouting to the woman that this is cheer practice, not charm school!"

"Some good all her charm has done her anyway." I think of the way she threw herself at Daddy yesterday.

"I do feel bad for her boys, but they are ornery. Mean as a pack of rattlesnakes."

"Yeah, she came by to pay her respects to Daddy."

"Oh Lord. Hey, Em, there's old Mr. Tomson."

"Poor guy. Is it true his nose was blown off in World War II?"

"Yeah, folks have been saying that he's getting crazier by the year. He's been walking River Road in the middle of the night."

Mr. Tomson is staring out at the creek and doesn't see us watching him. His skin is leathery in appearance, tanned a dark brown from his midday walks, and his thin gray hair stands straight up on his head in spots. His eyes have a slightly off kilter look about them, but what catches my eye is the blackened mass of dead skin where his nose should be.

Marcy comes out to get us and spots the man.

"Good afternoon, Mr. Tomson, it sure is a lovely day we're having. Can I get you a cool drink?"

"Kindly thanka, ma'am. My soldiers await. Hava seen my Bessie?"

"I haven't seen Bessie, sir."

Mr. Tomson nods and wanders down the boardwalk.

Chapter 14

I am hard-pressed to think of any better way to spend a Sunday meal. I am surrounded by the feminine backbones of this community enjoying sweet tea, laughter, and mighty fine food.

Earlier, Marcy and her mother-in-law, Ms. Hattie Hann, served up shrimp and grits with red-eye gravy, yellow squash casserole, fried green tomatoes, and pork barbecue. I have definitely eaten more than my belly can hold, but room must be made for blueberry buckle and pecan pie.

I start to clear dishes from the table, as Momma always taught me to do. Marcy puts her hand on my shoulder.

"Sug, there'll be plenty of dishes when ya'll get back to Indiana. Let us take care of you now."

Marcy and Hattie are as different in appearance as night and day, but they have like minds. Marcy is a freckly sort of pale and has long, bouncy frosted blond hair in the style of Farrah Fawcett. She seems on the taller side, but she adores wearing platform shoes with her bell bottoms. I've noticed a new "preppy" look in *Seventeen* magazine for fall. Somehow, I don't think Marcy will buy into that trend. It wouldn't seem right to see her dressed so conservatively.

Ms. Hattie Hann is a tiny, prim and proper black woman. Her skin is the color of freshly ground nutmeg and she has large expressive dark brown eyes in her tiny face. They go perfectly with her storytelling capabilities. She wears glasses that somehow magnify the size of her eyes even more. Hattie's husband, Curtis Sr., passed on a few years back, but Ms. Hat remains steadfast in the knowledge that she will be with him again in a better place. I didn't say hope because with Ms. Hat it is knowledge.

Abby and I sip our tea and pick at our desserts while Marcy and Lydia move to the kitchen to clean and prepare for the evening dinner rush. Ms. Hattie sits in the booth across from us, sipping her coffee.

"So what do y'all think of trees?" Ms. Hat seemingly stares right through me.

"I have no idea what you are talking about, Ms. Hat." I reply while glancing sideways at Abby.

"I often climbed trees as a little child, Ms. Hattie, and still do when given the opportunity."

"Spoken like a true daughter of the South, Abigail. You make your momma proud, I'm sure."

Ms. Hattie is speaking to Abby, but she's looking at me. I'm feeling uncomfortable and curious.

"Emma Cecille, it's about time you started learning your heritage. Your momma was a tender-hearted soul, so not much could be discussed when she was around. Well, dammit, you're old enough to know about your people. You've been in that God-forsaken, cold as a witch's teat north for too long now."

"I'm sorry, Ms. Hat, but I don't know . . ."

"I know ya don't know, girl, that's why I'm trying to tell ya. You see, to Southerners, a tree can be like an old friend."

"Fret did have Lydia tell us the story of Angel Oak last night, Ms. Hat."

"That's a good one, Em. I love that story." Abby puts her two cents in.

"Folklore, legend, it's all good, gals, but I'm looking for the truth. The facts. Trees are often the stuff of legend. Shoot, we even build roads around trees in these parts." Ms. Hat settles back into the cushioned seat of the booth. "Young gals, there are oak trees in the South that sprawl and spread like a spider spinning its web. Trees like that seem to reach straight up to the heavens. Your great grandma Lydia has a tree like that, Em."

I nod to show my agreement, but I still don't know where she's going with this. Abby appears equally confused.

"The same trees reaching to the heavens have roots embedded deep into the earth. That's how they stay around so long surviving hurricane and flood. I'd like to think those roots only search for strength and nourishment from the water and minerals found beneath the surface, but there's times I think those old deep roots can reach right down and touch the devil hisself.

"Gals, dontcha look upon me like I's crazy or sumpin. Some of these trees have a past associating with evil. Have ya heard of the strange fruit hanging from the trees in the deep South? Of course Negro men were lynched during days of slavery. Well, what about men wearing the damn Confederate uniform strung up in trees? During that second Great War, Negro men survived the Nazis only to be hanged on their own damn soil. Okay, the same trees harbored many an escaped slave during times of hardship. See what I'm saying, y'all, like most anything, I guess, good and evil can be served up fresh in the same place."

Abigail and I huddle a bit closer together on our side of the booth. Lydia and Marcy are chattering in the kitchen. Part of me wants to run and join them, but Ms. Hat has piqued my interest, in a morbid way.

"Well, there's love in the trees too. Angel Oak could be an example of that. What do ya know of your own family history, Emmy?" Ms. Hattie asks me while glancing over toward the kitchen.

"I don't know, Ms. Hat. I've only heard bits and parts here and there, usually from behind the kitchen door while the adults are talking."

Ms. Hat gets a kick out of that comment. "Lydia!" She calls to the kitchen.

"What is it, Hattie?" Lydia pokes her head out from behind the swinging kitchen door. "My hands are covered in flour. You don't need anything, do you?"

"I only need your permission to give these gals a little history lesson. It's about time Sug knew her people, her Southern people. Lord knows, she's well aware of those uptight, puritanical Methodists back home. Ain't much in the way of an interesting history there, I imagine."

I don't mind Ms. Hattie's dig at Daddy's family. She doesn't mean anything by it.

"Just keep in mind the age of the children you're speaking with, Hat. I don't want Abby's momma banning her from our gatherings . . . best keep those stories G rated." Lydia retreats to the kitchen leaving the door swinging in her wake.

Ms. Hattie smiles slyly. "That tree round by the river at Lydia's place, gals, that's a tree reaching straight up to the heavens. Even on that tragic day . . . well, it's been about thirty-four years ago now. Mmm, hmm. The time does fly. Seems like only yesterday when I cradled your little baby momma in my arms, Sug."

"You held Momma as a baby?"

"Course I did, Sug. Had only boys, myself, so I'd hold that beautiful little honey child every chance I'd get. Goodness, on that day, both Lydia's and your Grandma Rae's lives seemed to crumble like a dried up old biscuit. But I swear I saw that tree stretch right on up to touch the hand of God, pulling down His mantle and wrapping it securely 'round Lydia's shoulders. That tree drew us in almost, protected us from the storm raging around us."

"Ms. Hat, I mean no disrespect, but what on God's green earth are you talking about?"

"Sug, c'mon now. You mean to tell me you ain't never heard about Delilah?" Ms. Hat gives me a sort of wide-eyed mystical stare. I get the feeling she knows I've never heard of Delilah.

"Abby, do you know what she's talking about?"

"No idea. Who is Delilah, Ms. Hat?"

"Not who, little ladies, what," states Ms. Hat. "Ya did know, Sug, that your great granddaddy died in a drowning accident, right?"

Ms. Hat leans in close. I can smell the coffee and clove cigarettes on her breath. Supposedly she gave up smoking, but I can still smell those cloves. "I do know that much, Ms. Hat, but that's about it." I glance toward the kitchen door hoping this story doesn't get interrupted before it even starts.

"Abby and I would love to hear the story."

"Well, those ladies are boring the hell out of us working in the kitchen. We may as well entertain ourselves, huh?"

Ms. Hat motions to Marcy to refill our drinks as she passes by with water glasses for the tables.

"Mama, you stick to facts, ya hear?" Marcy says as she tops off our tea and Ms. Hat's coffee.

"Oh, gals, a mighty storm blew into these parts in September of '45. Your own momma, Sug, was just a wee child . . . still at Rae's teat, to be sure. Your great granddaddy, Shaef, and Lydia had just recently bought the River Road home from the senior Ridenours. Lydia and Shaef were working hard boarding up the place, preparing for the storm. I had left my Curtis at home with his daddy because RaeAnn thought I might could help with baby Meredith, your momma, while she helped her parents. Well, if ya know Rae at all, ya know she was doing a lot more worrying and carrying on than helping anyone.

"Your Grandma Rae is ten years my junior, and I did love that little movie star lookin' thing. I enjoyed helping her care for Meredith. She was awfully young to have a child, and Meredith's daddy was off serving in Europe. Besides Curtis was my youngest. He had his daddy and older brothers to help care for him."

"So my grandfather, my momma's daddy, was a soldier in World War II? Momma never even told me that." I am confused and amazed.

"Your momma was a sensitive soul, easily bogged down by disturbing thoughts. Let me tell the story, Sug. Don't you know it's rude to interrupt?"

Ms. Hat reaches across the table to squeeze my hand.

"Well now, Rae, Meredith and I were out on the veranda watching the storm develop. This was long before the storm warnings we have today, so no one could be quite sure how strong the storm might be. It had already been raining for quite some time when we received word that the bridge was washed out connecting Johns Island and River Road to James Island, the mainland and Charleston. The only way in or out at that point would be by boat. I wasn't too concerned for myself because, at that time, I lived just down the road a piece. My dear Curtis was keeping our boys safe, I was sure.

"The winds grew stronger and stronger as the day wore on. As evening approached, the rain became an absolute deluge. Shaef even spoke at that time about getting me home to my kinfolk. We had long before abandoned the veranda for the dry comfort of the house, but the wind whipped around and shook those boarded-up shutters something fierce. I was scared but took comfort in the confidence of Lydia and Shaef. They brewed good strong coffee, cooked cracklings on the kitchen fire, and lit a fire under that stone mantel to keep us warm. Rae laughed and joked with us while Mere slept quietly in the bassinet at her feet.

"Strange as it seems, from the river, we thought we heard a voice calling for RaeAnn. I can still hear that determined yet forlorn sound today . . . if I let myself think about it. It was the sound of a lonely, lovesick, and war torn man, ready to rest his eyes upon the face of his one and only love, Rae, and the child he'd only heard about in letters overseas.

RaeAnn, RaaaaeAaaan . . . The voice cried over the sound of the wind.

Well, Rae grabbed Meredith from the bassinet, and we all scrambled for the veranda, nearly knocking each other over in the process. Rae almost keeled over in fright because she thought her lover in the middle of the raging river was an apparition. The rain pounded us and the warm river water, sending up a fog into the cooler air of that storm. It looked as if Samson LaCouer was literally floating on top of the river. We knew a rowboat held him, logically, but could not see it.

"Did you know, Sug, that Samson LaCouer was your granddaddy?"

I shook my head in disbelief. The only grandfather I know of (on Momma's side) is Grandma Rae's current husband. I truly adore him, although we don't see them very often. I would occasionally hear my parents speaking quietly about Momma's family issues. I suppose the fact that Momma called Grandpa Tony by his first name made me realize he wasn't her daddy.

"Well, the relationship, liaison, tryst, romance . . . whatever you'd like to call it, was taboo back in that day, Sug. Do you know why, gals?" Ms. Hattie gives us a bug-eyed stare.

Abby and I shake our heads in unison.

"RaeAnn's a white gal last I checked, y'all. Although he was lighter than the lightest café au lait, Sam LaCouer was a Negro."

Abby and I look at one another in shock. Why hadn't anyone ever told me this before? Is it really true? Ms. Hat looks quite impressed with herself for throwing us into such a state with her story.

"Ms. Hattie, I've never heard anything about this before. Please go on. Please tell us more!" I am begging her. Why haven't I heard this before?

"I'll betcha ain't never asked, sugar baby. Aw, I ain't too sure you gals could handle hearing the rest. Ain't nothing like the truth, now. It's almost always stranger than fiction. Well, where were we?"

"On the veranda, in the storm . . ." Abby almost yells it. She is easily excited. "Emma's granddad was a black man? That's so exotic, so romantic!"

"That's right, that's right, of course." Ms. Hat begins.

"Hattie Hann, what sort of illicit gossip are you feeding into these young minds?" Lydia enters the dining room, removing her apron as she approaches.

I glance her way in admiration. It's hard to believe that she's almost seventy-five years old. Lydia says age is a state of mind, and her mind decided to stop aging at about fifty. She says at fifty a lady stops giving a damn about what everyone else thinks. She starts letting folks know what she thinks, for a change.

"Mama Hat, I appreciate you keeping the gals entertained while we were in the kitchen, but now we've gotta shoo them out to make way for the evening crowd."

"Ms. Marcy, she can't stop now. This story is unbelievable! I'm learning about relatives I never knew I had." I stand up and give Lydia my best pleading, puppy-dog eyes.

She, in turn, looks down into my face with her best "go to heck" eyebrow. But she is smiling.

"Let's make a deal. Sug, you and Abby set the tables for Ms. Marcy, and I'll bet Ms. Hattie will finish her story tomorrow night on the beach. That way your brothers can hear it too."

"Y'all best fill those boys in on what I told you in advance cause, Lord knows, I can't stand back tracking on a good story."

Abigail and I don't have to be told twice. I hug Ms. Hat after Abby, and we skip to the kitchen for plates, utensils and napkins. Tomorrow is July Fourth, and now I look forward to it for reasons other than the beach and fireworks.

Chapter 15

D id I dream about the little boat on the river in the storm? I don't know if I was dreaming or just waking and thinking about Ms. Hat's story. Grandma Rae was a bit of a maniac at Momma's funeral. She went on and on about Lydia and Momma ruining her life. I heard Daddy mutter about her being drunk. Too much vodka, that's what he'd said.

The shade is drawn in my little mahogany-floored bedroom, but the sunshine is fighting that window covering to get in. Streaks of yellow light play against the dark floorboards and on the pale blue wall opposite my bed, the big bed. This was Momma's bed growing up. Never have I been in a more comfortable bed. It is elevated four feet off the floor by a frame made of beautiful cherry wood with four posts. Maybe this is how a princess feels.

I can hear the window air conditioner kick on in the hallway, and the cool air reaches my room almost immediately, inviting me to snuggle back into the soft, cool cotton sheets. I burrow my head into the fluffy down pillow and admire the brown of my suntanned arm against the pure white matelasse blanket.

There's only one wall decoration in the room. It's really all the little room needs with the big bed, an equally large cherry dresser with antique pitcher and washbowl atop, the small dressing table in the corner, and the pale blue window coverings. Lydia said Momma found the wall decoration at the market in Charleston when she was seven or eight years old. Momma simply fell in love with the tiny pair of ceramic "wooden" shoes, made in Holland. Momma's favorite color was blue. The little shoes are a cream color with a delicate blue tulip pattern across their tops.

As I gaze at the shoes dangling from a brown thread on the lone nail, I say a little prayer to Momma and to God.

I tell Momma how much I love her and miss her, but I thank God for my family- the family He has chosen to leave here with me. I ask God to keep Daddy safe while we are away from him. I wonder to myself and then prayerfully ask Momma why she never told me about her real daddy. I seem to hear her reply. She was not aware that she had limited time. She would have shared these stories with me in due time.

Warm tears soak the downy pillow.

Chapter 16

E m . . . Em . . ."
    I wake up to see Fret peeking around my bedroom door.

"Oh, hey Fret, c'mon in." I smile at my little brother. I look at his skin color, now wondering how closely it might resemble my own. Fret's getting older now and becoming independent, but we were once almost inseparable.

One Christmas Eve, back home, the snow fell outside my window, and Fret and I cuddled up together in my four poster bed. Watching the snow fall softly outside through the sheers covering my window was a magical sight. We fought sleep, tooth and nail, trying to stay up long enough to catch Santa in the act. I must have been about seven or eight and Fret four or five at the time. The radio station promised to play Christmas carols all night. We thought this would help us stay awake. The later it got, the more they played slow instrumental versions. I've been through enough Christmas Eve masses to know. O Holy Night, Silent Night and O Tannenbaum in instrumental can knock out even the most faithful caroling enthusiast.

That is one of my favorite Christmas memories, and unfortunately Fret doesn't even remember it.

"Watcha doing, Fretty?

He climbs up onto the big bed.

"Lydia sent me to wake up your sleepy head. It's July Fourth. Uncle Ty and Aunt Katie will be here soon to take us out to Kiawah."

"Where's Jay?"

"He got up early. Couldn't sleep another wink. He's been out fishing off the pier all morning." Fret hops off the bed and throws open the shade. He lifts the window and yells out to Jay. "Hey, rain in the face, you catch anything?"

I look out the window too. Jay motions for us to join him outside.

A few moments later, Fret and I race down the front steps, past the shady oak and out to the end of the pier. Lydia and Granddad call to us to be careful as we pass them on the veranda. The large oak helps them enjoy filtered morning sun. When I turn and look back at them from the pier, I notice dappled sunlight hitting the house, the covered veranda and their faces. On the pier the sun shines hot and strong.

"Y'all need to get ready for your bike ride and beach day."

"I'm putting things away, Lydia. We'll be up in a minute." Jay watches us run down the pier and yells to Lydia and Granddad, "definitely won't be catching anything now!"

Jay bends over his tackle box. His thick brown hair has taken on blond highlights this summer. The blond streaks are exaggerated against his tan face making his blue eyes stand out more than ever. Jay is short for his age and all the girls think he's the cutest boy in school. This would include many of my friends.

"Catch anything?" Fret asks again.

"Nah, not much luck. The tide's moving out though. It will be a perfect day at the beach. Hey, Em, Lydia said Ms. Hat has a story for us tonight?"

"Yeah, she does. I can't wait to hear the rest of it. I'm supposed to fill you in on everything she's told us so far. You won't believe it!"

"You can tell us on the beach."

"What story? Tell us the story!" Fret hops from foot to foot, barefoot and excited on the hot pier.

"It's about a storm when Momma was a baby and her daddy came home from war to see her." I like knowing more than Jay about something.

"Tell us now, Em. Is it about Grandpa Tony? He was a soldier?"

"Fret, do you have to use the bathroom? Stop that jumping. I don't know about Grandpa Tony. He's not Momma's daddy." I am smart.

"Everybody knows that, brainless."

Jay says this in the sarcastic way of a big brother.

"Momma would not have called him 'Tony' if he were her real father. Fret, settle down. We've gotta go. Emma will tell us the story on the beach."

Jay balances his tackle box and fishing pole while steering Fret in the direction of the house.

"We call Lydia 'Lydia' and she really is our great grandma," Fret sticks his tongue out at Jay.

I kick at the back of Jay's knee as he walks away causing his leg to buckle. He grabs me and puts me in a headlock, dropping his pole and tackle box with a clatter. He digs his knuckles into the top of my head, rubbing back and forth.

"Noogie patrol! Tell us something we don't know, Em!" he yells.

"Stoooop!" I elbow him in the ribs and chase after Fret. Suddenly I stop and put my right hand on my hip in a perfect "told you so" pose.

The boys notice my stance and stop in their tracks.

"Momma's daddy was named Samson LaCouer, and he was a black man."

Chapter 17

The sun is setting over the western end of Kiawah. We are meeting around the beach bonfire to chat and listen to the rest of Ms. Hattie's story. The fireworks are set to begin at 9:30 down the beach a bit, in front of the inn. Ms. Hat motions for us to join her near the fire.

The air is still tonight. The smoke curls straight up off the fire, keeping the mosquitoes at bay for now. The wood crackles and pops as it burns. Sounds of laughter and music travel along the water's edge to us from the party at the inn. The waves meet the shore with a muffled crash. That is a sound I never tire of hearing. I miss that sound almost as much as these people when I'm back in Indiana.

Sometimes I sit quietly in my room at home, on my bed with the bright yellow bedspread that Momma gave me. I pull a large conch shell off the bookcase and listen to the ocean there. Each time I am amazed that the roar of the waves can be heard within that shell. I bet if a doctor had an x-ray machine that examined one's soul, he could shine his light right through me. A big Atlantic Ocean wave would come crashing right out of me. The doctor would be knocked over backward with the force of my wave. He'd be thrown upside down, disoriented even, and come sputtering up to the surface laughing. He'd turn off his x-ray machine and simply say, "This child has a real love of the ocean."

Jay and Fret are jogging down the beach from the inn. Jay calls to his friends, telling them he'll meet them back there for the fireworks. Fret chases a wayward ghost crab.

"Look, Em. I caught one this time without a pinch!"

Fret walks towards me holding the ghost crab by the back in his outstretched hand.

"That little guy is out early tonight. It's not even dark yet." I inspect the creature held before me. "He's cute."

With that comment, Fret drops the crab. The creature scampers in my direction, claws snapping as he moves. I squeal and jump out of the way which tickles the boys.

"You are a wimp, Miss Emma Phend." Jay says.

I punch him in the back as he walks towards the bonfire. Fret darts away from the punch I send in his direction.

"C'mon now, y'all. Gather round here. Ms. Hat just don't have that kind of energy. I might doze off soon."

"Can I get you anything from the cooler, Hat?"

Lydia brushes her lips across the top of my head as she passes by. She leaves the smell of Chanel No. 5 in her wake. Even after a day at the beach, she can still manage to smell good.

"A Coke is fine, Lydia. Thanka kindly, dear friend."

Jay and Fret sit down by Granddad, Uncle Ty and Curtis. Kona inserts herself comfortably between the boys. I gather Ben onto my lap and cuddle in between Ms. Marcy and Aunt Katy. Lydia settles into a lawn chair next to Ms. Hat.

"Now where did I leave off, Sug?"

The fire dances in the reflecting pools of Ms. Hattie's glasses, making her appear magical . . . or creepy.

"The storm was raging, Ms. Hat, and Lydia and Shaef and Grandma Rae just spotted Samson LaCouer in his boat."

"Hmm . . . some young folk do listen to their elders." Ms. Hat chuckles. "May I, Lydia? It is your story after all."

"I've never told it very well. Too close to home. Please continue, Hat."

"We was right there in front of that River Road home y'all know and love. That was over thirty years ago."

"I remember like it was yesterday," Lydia sighs.

She and Granddad exchange a look across the fire in the waning light of the day.

"The storm seemed to be reaching fever pitch. The wind swirled and howled all around us. Samson LaCouer was a fine young buck of a man in that day. He was hard working and industrious, as well. Any Negro gal in the parish would've been overjoyed to take him as her husband. Samson, however, was cursed with the love of that little

RaeAnn Shaefer. That was the rumor round these parts always. Seemed like she had him under a spell. He'd of done anything for that gal.

"They couldn't marry. But Sam wrote to Rae from Europe, where he was fighting the war, saying they could move to Paris and marry after the war. When Samson heard Rae had birthed his daughter, Meredith, he was more determined than ever to make their family situation legal. He fought for this country with great valor and dignity but had grown to resent the fact that he couldn't marry his true love due to the color of his skin.

"RaeAnn stood on the veranda cradling Meredith and crying out to Samson, seemingly oblivious to the storm.

Saaaaaaamsooon! I have your baby girl here. Meredith. Please come to shore.

"Most likely Samson could not see Meredith, but Rae held her out toward him in the rain. In his excitement Samson LaCouer shifted in such a way that the damned skiff flipped right over. He was gone in an instant.

"I grabbed your momma from Rae. She went racing down to the swollen river screaming his name. The river lapped all the way up to the Oak. Lydia and Shaef ran after Rae, fighting to remain upright in the soaked grass. Even over the sound of the wind, I could hear Shaef and Lydia arguing. Lydia held Rae back to keep her from jumping into the raging river. Gently, I bounced Meredith on the veranda to keep her quiet. Shaef kicked off his shoes and dove into the river. My heart raced as I held your momma close.

"The little boat whirled around in the wind as if caught up in a waterspout. Shaef swam out to about where Samson fell overboard. He dove down beneath the surface. Rae was wailing and moaning beneath the Oak. I could hear Lydia telling her to quit carrying on so. That was not helping matters at all. Shaef surfaced, gagging and spitting water from his mouth. I could barely make him out, but his actions were determined. He dove down again. That time he came up with a good grip on Samson.

"Rae wailed.

Saaaamsoooon . . . Daddeeeeee . . .

"Samuel Shaefer struggled, obviously, but began the swim to shore. Well, that skiff kicked up out of the water like an object possessed. It caught the wind and a wave and *Poom!* I hear that sound like it was yesterday.

"Mere whimpered softly in my arms.

"Rae screamed.

Mother, get them!!! Get them!!!

"Lydia pushed RaeAnn under the protection of the Oak and cradled her like a newborn baby.

We don't need anymore death on this day, Rae. No more death.

"The rain did not stop, and the river surged. I watched as the water lapped at their feet. Lydia and Rae kept watch for what seemed an eternity under the nurturing canopy of that tree.

"When Lydia and Rae finally came to the house, Meredith was screaming her lungs out. I told Rae that the baby needed a good nursing. I thought that giving of nourishment to the child might calm Rae a bit, as well. RaeAnn looked at the baby, at me and then at Lydia.

My teats have turned as dry and cold as my heart on this day. What is my reason for living? It has ceased to exist with the coming of this God forsaken storm to this God forsaken home.

"Lydia looked very briefly taken aback, but she had been dealing with her daughter's drama for quite some time. I'm sure she thought Rae's distraught feelings would pass. Lydia crossed over to me and took Mere from my arms. The baby quieted immediately. Lydia ever so gently nuzzled Mere's cheek and turned to Rae.

I know this is painful. I too suffer in this loss. But this, this gorgeous child is your reason for living.

"Rae looked her mother coldly in the face.

Perhaps a child is your raison d'être, but it certainly ain't mine.

"With that, Rae walked out the back door of the River Road home.

"It was a week before the waters receded enough to search for the bodies. Ironically, Sam Shaefer's body was found immediately, washed up near the old Guerreville site, but Samson LaCouer's body was never found.

"That was just before the National Weather Service started giving storms names, but folks up and down the Carolina coast called that one Delilah. Delilah had not come in search of just their strength, their manhood. No, the two Sams displayed strength and manhood in all its glory. She had come for their lives."

As if on cue, the first rocket shoots into the sky from the inn. The red tail hangs behind the giant firecracker. With a loud *Boom*, it opens up in a blaze of red streamers whistling over the Atlantic.

Chapter 18

T he best part of July Fourth is actually July fifth. We always spend
the night at the beach house owned by the island's Turkish
developers. Because of the work they do on the island, both Uncle Ty
and Curt Hann have access to this old run-down beach house.

There's a large dormer room on the third level with wide-open
views of the Atlantic and four sets of bunk beds set up end to end. I
look down to see Ben sleeping on the bottom bunk next to mine. Kona
is curled up at his feet. I pat the dog and kiss Ben on the cheek before
heading downstairs.

I quietly make my way through the house. I hear Aunt Katie
humming in the kitchen on the main level. I call to her being careful not
to wake the Hanns or Lydia and Granddad.

"Aunt Katie, I'm going out to the beach. Ben is still sleeping."

"Thanks, Em. I'll go on up and lie down with him a spell. Those
brothers of yours had me up awfully early."

"They out fishing?"

"Of course! Enjoy your morning, Emma."

"See you after while."

I walk down the rickety wooden steps and onto the boardwalk
leading through the tall bank of sea oats and out to the beach. Kiawah
actually faces South because of the way the mainland curves at this
point. The beach house is on the western end of the island, so I look
towards the inn to the east to see the sun rising at the far end of the
island.

The tide is low as I walk out to the hard-packed sand at the water's
edge. Bending over to stretch the backs of my legs, I notice a living
starfish caught in a tidal pool. I walk over and place my hand in the

warm water, reaching to grab the funny creature. There is ticklish pleasure in saving the life of a starfish. An egret looks up from his own fishing excursion but is not bothered by my presence and goes right back to his work. The pale brown, bumpy starfish gently curls his rays around my palm as I lift him out of the water. I lay it flat on my palm, and the creature uses his many small feet to tickle my hand. Trying to escape, perhaps.

"I won't hurt you buddy."

Taking the starfish to the spot where the waves crash calmly ashore, I place it in the moving water. My brothers and I have been on starfish patrol here for a very long time. Momma taught each of us to save the creatures we find trapped in the tide pools.

"You're brown as a berry, Sug."

I was so focused on saving the starfish that I didn't even notice Lydia and Granddad sitting near the shoreline. They hold still-steaming mugs of coffee, and a fishing pole is propped against Granddad's chair.

"I kept quiet as a church mouse inside thinking y'all were asleep." I hug each of them from behind, breathing in the smell of the combination of salt air and their soapy-clean skin. "This is my favorite morning of the summer."

"I'm sure your brothers feel the same way, Sug. They took off a short time ago to meet some of the Feegan boys down at the river to fish." Lydia tilts her head back in my embrace, resting her head on my arm briefly.

"Tide's fixing to turn. Should be good fishing down there." Granddad gives me a wink.

"The dolphins will be fishing too. Won't they, Granddad?"

"Pretty much a guarantee, Sug."

"That was quite a story last night, wasn't it?" Lydia says and stares out to sea.

I settle down next to them in a hurdler's stretch.

Granddad motions in my direction. "Now, if I got down there in that position, it'd take a military platoon to get me back up."

"I have just one question . . . okay a million, but one right now, Lydia." I tell her while bending out over my leg, stretching my chest towards my kneecap.

"Mm-hmm."

"What does raison d'être mean?"

"Oh, Sug . . ." Lydia laughs out loud. "That's French for 'reason for being,' your purpose, right?"

"So Grandma Rae just didn't give a damn about Momma? Pardon my French, but that's just not right." I feel an ache deep in my heart for Momma.

"I've said it before, Sug, and as God is my witness I'm sure I'll say it again. Some folks learn and draw strength from hardships, adversity, and other folks let it crush them like the waves pounding this here beach."

"Lord only knows why that is," interjects Granddad. "Your great grandmother here has always amazed me. It is almost as if adversity fuels her, giving her fire and strength to live. That fire drew me to her."

"Well, most people can't stand a Pollyanna." Lydia squeezes Granddad's arm. "Your Grandma Rae has faced her fair share of bad luck and maybe not handled it very well, Sug, but she's still kin. She has grown a bit and is decent to you kids. The proverbial prodigal son. Don't let these old stories alone shape your view of a woman who's been nothing but kind to you."

"How can I not, Lydia? I want Momma back right now. I want to hug her and tell her how much I love her even though her own mother didn't. I want to talk to her about her real daddy. Why didn't she ever tell us that we are all part black?" I choke on my words a bit as this anger threatens to strangle me.

"Your momma considered herself blessed, Sug. That's the trick. She had her own raison d'être all figured out. She never knew Samson LaCouer, and she certainly didn't look black. I believe she didn't know what good it would do to discuss it." Lydia seems to smile at the thought.

"Did Samson LaCouer have family here? Did she ever know any of them?"

"Oh, Sug, you'd have to understand the times we were living in. It's hard enough in this day and age for mixed couples like Marcy and Curtis. Samson had only his mother here, and she moved to France immediately following the drownings. She was a lovely woman. I considered her a friend, but we lost contact years ago."

"You'd best get on with your run there, Sug." Granddad places a protective arm around Lydia. "You ladies can talk about this any old time. The dolphins won't be there feeding if the tide comes in too far."

Chapter 19

R ight now I feel like I'm trying to breathe underwater. The air feels that heavy this morning. There's a steady breeze hitting my face as I head west down the beach to the river. I like to run close to the water's edge where the sand is still firm. I keep my eye on tide pools for creatures in need of my assistance. Once I found a baby hammerhead shark trapped in a tide pool. I was scared to death, but I picked it up by its leathery tail and carried it out into the surf.

Just a little exercise is all I'm getting out here. I usually can't take a serious run on the beach. Too many distractions. I also watch for loggerhead turtle tracks. The mother loggerheads come ashore in the summer months to lay their eggs up in the softer sand of the dunes and oat grass. Last summer we were out on the beach late one night and saw a mother loggerhead come ashore to nest. Daddy thought there was a log out in the water. Jay shone his flashlight across the shoreline and there she was! We turned out all the flashlights and sat quietly for fifteen minutes or so, watching her lumber ashore in the moonlight. It was amazing. Momma said in all her years of living down here, she had never seen such a thing. Even Ben watched quietly.

I'm just running with the river in mind, knowing I will stop for a chat with the boys to see what's been caught. As I come closer to the river, the tide has created huge warm pools away from the shoreline. I remove my Nikes and socks to wade barefoot in the soothing water. Occasionally, a blue crab scampers nearby, and hermit crabs teeter across my feet in their funny sideways crawl. I run my shoes up and place them on the beach where the eventual incoming tide won't reach. I go back into the tide pool and sit right down in the balmy water, running shorts, t-shirt and all. I lean back and tilt my face towards the hot sun.

As I lay there quietly, I can hear the boys at the river, laughing and carrying on about Lord only knows what.

"Hey, Emma."

My stomach does a little cartwheel as I turn to see the boy staring down at me.

"Hey." I respond, realizing that I'm sitting (okay, lying) in a tide pool, fully clothed.

"I'm Blake Feegan. I met you the other morning after mass with Abby Doyle."

"I know. It's nice to meet you again." I half smile up at the tall boy with the sun-bleached hair while becoming aware of the fact that my back side is most likely covered in sand. I can't possibly stand up to greet him properly.

Instead, the boy plops down in the warm water next to me.

"I'm sorry I looked at you strangely the other day, but I felt like I had seen you before. Well, when I just saw you running down the beach, I realized you were the girl my brother and I saw running on River Road. How often do you run?"

"I don't know, just whenever I feel like it." I'm not sure why he has such an interest in my running habits.

"My dad would like me to run more. He says it would help me in tennis and football, in any sport really, but I'd much rather go fishing. That's what my brother and I were doing when we saw you on River Road."

He reaches forward to grab a hermit crab from the water.

"Now that is some shell, little fella."

The crab ducks as far as possible back into the shell. Blake holds the crab in front of me. Its shell is a brilliant blue and gray, unlike any I've ever seen. Blake lightly punches me in the arm and jumps up. He runs the crab to the surf and looks back at me.

"I'm sorry, Emma. I've been fishing with your brothers all morning. I guess I feel like I know you. That and your uncle helped my dad build our house here on the island. And Abby talks about you all the time."

"Yeah. She talks a lot." I smile at him, "but you just might have her beat, Blake Feegan!"

I get to my feet and start brushing the sand from my clothes and the backs of my brown legs.

"I'll race you to the river!" I call to him and take off running in a dead sprint.

"Hey! You got a head start!"

Blake yells this from behind me, but he is quick to catch me and sticks out his tongue while racing past.

"I thought you said you don't run?" I yell after him.

"Not usually, not without a football or tennis racquet in my hand!"

Chapter 20

B lake is ahead of me all the way to the river's edge. He is bent over, breathing hard, as I join the guys.

"Hola, rain in the face," states Jay flatly as I approach.

"Hey, it's the little running girl." Blake's older brother says this in our direction from his seat between my brothers on the riverbank.

"Emma, this is my jerk of a big brother, Hank." Blake motions towards his brother.

"And he means that in only the fondest of ways," Hank adds sarcastically.

Despite their mocking behavior, I can see the brothers have a good relationship and are only messing around.

"It's nice to meet you, Hank. Have y'all had any luck down here this morning?"

"Jay snapped a line, Em," Fret begins, "We're not sure what was on there, but it took his bait, half his line and swam straight out to sea!"

"Just about took me with it."

Jay is focused on the water.

"Look guys, right here along the bank. That a black tip, Hank?"

As Jay motions, there is a splash right up next to the sandy shore. The shark turns quickly and darts back into deeper water.

"That thing was pretty good sized." Blake moves in for a closer look, but the shark is gone.

"Probably a four-footer or so. I'd like to see it strung up on one of our lines, eh Jay?"

I can tell that Hank and Jay have become fast friends.

"There ya go, Em. I'm sure that's what you came down to the river to see . . ." Jay points upriver, away from the ocean, in the direction of the opposite bank.

There, a school of dolphins can be seen hunting for their breakfast.

"C'mon, Em, Blake, let's get closer." Fret springs up and moves inland along the tidal ridge created by the changing river.

I follow along behind Fret and Blake. Fret is chattering away and pointing. A snowy egret swoops down to my right to snatch a scampering hermit crab away from its naked and now pointless search for a new home.

The Kiawah River sweeps around the island at this spot called Captain Sam's Inlet. Seabrook Island is on the western side of the inlet. At low tide the beach seems to jut out into the sea a quarter mile. The muddy banks of the marshland are expansive on the river side of the island.

A flock of pelicans sweep low over the shallow river waters. It amazes me how such an awkward looking, big-beaked bird can look so graceful and majestic in the air.

Fret continues to lead us, following the dolphins as they feed.

"Remember, Fret, Curt told us to stay back a few feet from the water, so they aren't afraid to feed on the bank." I remind my little brother.

"I am back, and they're not bothered at all. Look!"

He's right. What appear to be a mother and baby corral a school of fish right up onto the riverbank. Fish are flopping everywhere. The dolphins are close enough for us to hear their happy squeaks.

"I've never seen them do this so close." Blake says.

"This is the greatest." I add.

"So cool." Fret's smile stretches from ear to ear.

It is hot. Sweat drips between my shoulder blades. The sky is perfectly blue above us with a spot of puffy cumulus clouds here and there. The river is clear blue-green, more deep blue where the clouds cast their shadow. The dolphins seem pleased as they put on this amazing show just for us.

"I wish I could live down here year-round. You're lucky, Blake. Man, I'd be fishing every day!" Fret jumps as one of the dolphins splashes the shoreline.

"That's great in theory, Fret, but we do have school and chores and sports- thank God for that- to keep us busy during the school year."

"Guess it'd be hard to sit in school all day with that sun beaming in all the time."

"Fret, don't act like the sun never shines back home." I suddenly feel defensive.

"In winter, sometimes it's cloudy and gray for weeks. You know it's true, Em."

"In spring too, actually."

"Y'all hear that?" Blake asks.

"Was it thunder?" I look at the sky over the far end of Seabrook. "Look at that storm!"

"It came out of nowhere." Fret is looking in the same direction.

"They have a tendency to do that around here," Blake begins, "C'mon. Let's help the guys load up the gear."

Fret, Blake and I run back to the spot where we left Hank and Jay fishing. They're nearly done loading things into the cart behind Hank's bike. The rain looks like a screen between the clouds and the water. The other boys hop on their bikes while Blake motions for me to ride with him.

"C'mon, Emma. We don't have much time. That storm is coming in quickly."

"You got her, Blake?" Jay calls to us through the now swirling wind.

"We're fine, Jay!" I call. "Stay with Frettie, okay?"

Jay gives me a thumbs up and rides to catch up with Hank and Fret. I run over to grab my shoes and socks from the beach while Blake rides behind me. I stuff my socks in my shoes, climb on the bike seat, and hang on to Blake's shirt with my free hand. Blake holds onto the handlebars while straddling the bike, keeping it steady.

"I don't see any lightning out there," he says. "That's a good sign, but let's go. We're going to get soaked!"

The raindrops feel cool against my skin. I'm hanging on tight to the back of Blake's shirt as he pedals fast to catch the others. Like the blowing windstorm sand of one of Jay's Louis L'Amour novels, the rain pelts our skin. I feel fully alive. Suddenly, I laugh uncontrollably.

"Are you laughing or crying?" Blake asks in an alarmed voice.

"Oh my goodness, Blake Feegan. I can't stop laughing. This is crazy . . . this is fun!"

Now Blake laughs along with me.

"Good. I wouldn't know what to do if you were crying."

"This rain is blinding. Can you see?"

"Not really, but I can feel the sand under the tires. I've been caught in these storms before."

The rain lets up a bit as we reach the boardwalk leading to the beach house.

"Blake! Your brother rode up to the inn walkway. He said you'd better get home quick 'cause your momma will be worried."

"Thanks, Fret. You okay, Em?" Blake asks as I slide off his bike.

"Yeah. Thanks for the ride."

"Unlike your brothers, I would not leave you stranded in that storm." He takes a punch at Fret's arm.

"Man, I was lucky to get my own scrawny butt back here." Fret shakes his rear end in front of us and heads for the boardwalk.

"See ya, Em. Maybe you'd like to play tennis sometime?"

Even through the rain, Blake's eyes are bright.

"I'm not much of a tennis player."

"I'm a pretty good teacher."

"Okay. Thanks for the ride, Blake."

"See ya later."

He gives me a quick hug. Only because that's the type of boy he is. The hugging, generous type, I mean. The rain picks up again as I run up the boardwalk.

Chapter 21

As I approach the beach house, I can see that Fret is in a head-lock. It is Claudette Jenkins' youngest boy, David, wrestling with my little brother. Jay and Whitey, Ms. Jenkins' older boy, encourage them. From his bent position, Fret is yelling and pummeling David's ribcage.

"What is going on?" I ask.

"Ah, let 'em fight, Emma. That's what boys do. You're such a prissy little goody-two-shoe girl. You'd never understand," Whitey retorts.

Jay rolls his eyes in my direction while shouting encouragement to Fret.

Fret tries to wriggle his way out of the head-lock, but David holds him tight.

"Em," Fret cries, "this little jerk called me a monkey. Told me I should go back to the jungle!"

Fret gives David a good punch in the gut, and he loosens his grip. As David moves to punch Fret back, I wedge myself between the boys, pushing David in the process.

"David Alan Dingbat Young, what exactly do you mean by that statement? You wanna tell me exactly what you mean by that?"

David is two years younger than me and a year older than Fret, but he's as tall as I am. We look each other square in the eye.

"I mean y'all are a bunch of jungle bunny lovin' Yankees!"

"You are called Dingbat for a reason, David," Jay warns while snickering. "You do not want to make her mad!"

Jay and Whitey laugh hard. They are both bent over holding their stomachs. Fret doesn't want them to see him cry. I can tell by the way he clenches his fists, he is very upset. Fortunately the rain masks his tears.

"Well, you know what you are, David Alan Dingbat Young, besides a dingbat?" I stand as tall as I possibly can. I push him again on the narrow boardwalk. "You are the most ignorant, white-trash talking cracker I have ever seen!"

I give the scrawny, blond boy one more push, and his eyes are huge as he falls backwards off the boardwalk. He lands flat in the middle of a prickly briar patch. He screams in pain. I grab Fret's hand, and we make a run for the house.

"Way to go, Em," Jay says. He and Whitey move to help David out of the briar patch.

"I hope a damn bobcat gets you! Jerk." Of course, I must have the last word.

I hear the older boys' laughter as Fret and I round the wild hedge on the front side of the house. David can be heard cussing and crying from the painful heat of the briars embedded in his skin.

"What in the Sam hell is going on out there, y'all?"

It's Granddad calling from the screened porch of the beach house. The adults are gathered around the large wooden table there. Ms. Jenkins is wearing her large sunglasses. Inside and in the rain! She appears to be holding an ice pack on her shoulder.

"My boys bothering y'all out there?" She asks in a weary voice.

I can barely hear her. And upon closer inspection, I see the reason for her sunglasses. The camouflage isn't working. Ms. Jenkins has a deep purple-black bruise extending out of the top of her blouse where her shoulder meets the slope of her neck. The same color can be seen through the heavy makeup on her face beneath her right eye. Oh, and above her eye too. The large sunglasses need to be even larger to mask that shiner.

Lydia glances in our direction but nods to Aunt Katy.

"What happened out there?" Aunt Katy asks while steering us to the front room. Ben is there playing with his train set.

"Little disagreement with Ms. Jenkins boys is all," I tell her.

"Hey, Ben," says Fret. "Can I play trains with you?"

At the sight of his cousin, Fret has seemingly forgotten the incident outside. The boys play together on the floor.

"What happened to Ms. Jenkins?" I ask Aunt Katy.

"Oh, nothing for you to worry about. She had a little visit from David and Whitey's daddy early this morning." She whispers, "Apparently he was angry and drunk. Neither is good, but together . . . a recipe for disaster."

"Is she okay?"

"Just keep it quiet, Em. Lydia and Travis will make sure she's alright."

Chapter 22

The storm has passed, and I'm bored inside watching the boys play with trains. I pass through the screened porch on my way back outside.

"Where you headed, Sug?" Marcy asks.

"I'm going to see what the guys are doing outside."

"They been out there all morning," Ms. Jenkins says distractedly. Her words sound slow and slurred.

"Em, you tell 'em I'll skin their hides if they're making trouble."

I'm thinking enough hides have been skinned today.

"Sure, Ms. Jenkins. I'll check on them."

Lydia gives me a weary look while waving me outside.

"Go on, Sug. It's okay. The boys are fine, I'm sure."

As I open the battered side door onto the deck, I notice a large spider perched in the middle of its web. The web stretches probably two feet across the corner rails of the deck. A chill runs down my spine as I put as much distance as possible between me and that spider. I should ask Curtis what sort of spider that is.

The boys are sitting in the sand on the beach, shirts off and bare-footed.

"Hey."

"Oh, dammit all, the mean one is back," David says, glancing my way.

"Didn't I warn you not to provoke her?" Jay asks.

"C'mon, y'all. She was only sticking up for the brownie." Whitey says with a smirk and lies back in the sand.

With difficulty I resist the urge to kick sand in his face and instead sit down next to David. "David Alan, I'm sorry I pushed you into the prickly plant. I really didn't mean to do it."

"Yeah, right," Jay says with a laugh.

"S'okay," David says.

"Is our stupid mama still up there at the house?" asks Whitey.

"Don't call your mama stupid," I scold. "Maybe you're lucky to have a mama."

"Ah, point taken," says Whitey. "But really, she's stupid."

Now David jumps up in defense of their mama. "She ain't stupid, you ass!"

David kicks sand in his older brother's face, and, suddenly, the two are wrestling.

"Take it back, take it back!"

David is crying and flailing his arms, missing his brother every time.

"Cut it out, guys." Jay moves toward them.

Whitey pins David's hands at his side. David kicks at his older brother while crying.

"She ain't stupid, White one, she ain't."

David falls on the ground, crying and covering his face with his hands.

"It ain't worth it. Jay, let's hit the surf again. The waves out there are calling my 'King of Bodysurfing' name."

I sit next to David as the others run off into the ocean.

"Go away, Em. Just go away. You're mean and full of yourself. You're a know-it-all, and I hate you."

He keeps his head down, buried in his arms.

"What happened, David? What happened to your mama?"

"She is stupid, Em, but I ain't ever admitted that to Whitey. She had to know my daddy would be at the inn last night. He's a fireman. He always helps with the fireworks. Why does she show up throwing herself at the tennis guy?"

"What tennis guy?" I begin, but then I remember, "Oh, the new pro at Kiawah."

"Yeah, he don't give a damn about Mama. I seen him with three different ladies last night alone. Mama was drunk. Throwing herself at him. Daddy saw her."

David wipes his nose with his bare arm. He sits up straighter. He appears relieved. Relieved to tell someone about this, even if it's me.

"Aren't your parents divorced?" I ask, "Why does your daddy care what your mama does?"

"Just likes to see her cry, I guess. He's always getting mad and hitting her. Ain't no rhyme or reason."

"Did your daddy get in trouble? Did anyone see him do this?"

"Hell no, Em. He ain't stupid. Waited 'til he had her alone. He ain't stupid."

We are both quiet for a moment. The day has become warm and humid again, and I envy the boys in the water. The tide is in, and the waves lap at our toes.

"Well, David Alan, I'm sorry I pushed you. But, please don't call my little brother names again. Okay?" I give him a light punch in the arm.

"You'd better not tell nobody you seen me crying then."

He punches me back, a little harder.

"Ow," I hold my arm. "Sounds like a deal."

"Deal!"

David shouts this while leaping up to jump an incoming wave.

Chapter 23

We celebrated Jay's fifteenth birthday last evening with a real southern barbecue and Lydia's butterscotch pie. That's Jay's favorite, and he'd take that over cake any day of the week. Even though Lydia does make an amazing red velvet. Uncle Ty and Curtis were in charge of the barbecue while the ladies tended to the other dishes. Abby came back over last night to spend the night with us at the beach.

There appears to be no threat of rain today. That's what I thought yesterday though. Abby, Fret, Ben and I run barefoot down the hot boardwalk to the beach. As soon as we exit the boardwalk, we land in the even hotter sand. We jump, skip and scamper down to the cooler hard-pack. I hold Ben's hand from the boardwalk to the water's edge. He runs ahead and jumps chest-first into an incoming wave.

"Are you supposed to let him do that, Em?" Abby asks.

Ben spits water from his mouth and smiles after being knocked over backwards by the wave. Fret dives head-first into a wave farther out. Ben cheers him from the knee-deep water.

"Shoot, Abby, he's fine. He's out in this water with his daddy almost every day of the summer. He's not even four yet and can swim like a fish." I tell her.

"As long as you're taking full responsibility."

"Quit being such a worry wart, Abs. Let's join him!"

I run and grab Ben, swing him around in the air before crashing together into the next wave.

"Where's Jay, Fret?" I call to my little brother.

"I think he went down to the inn. Probably looking for girls."

"What are we? Chopped liver?" asks Abby.

"Oh my Lord, Ab, I'm his sister, for goodness sake, and you're too young for him!"

"Well, I'm already wearing a B cup bra, Em. Some ninth grade girls can't even say that." She sticks out her chest as she says this. "Mama just bought me this string bikini too. My favorite color, purple. Whatcha think?"

"I think you're strutting around like an over-proud peacock. C'mon, Ben. Let's go out a little farther."

I grab hold of Ben and splash water in the direction of my best friend. She definitely gets more looks from the boys with her B-cup status than me and my flat chest.

She may be the boy crazy one, but I do notice Blake Feegan, his brother Hank, Whitey and David walking with Jay down the beach.

"C'mon, Abby!" Ben calls as he climbs on my back.

Together we head out to sea.

"Any sign of pirates on the horizon there, matey?" I ask this of Fret as we plough into the waist-deep water, letting the waves wash over us. I concentrate on planting my feet firmly as each wave approaches. I don't want to get knocked back into the water with the little guy on my back.

"I see, I see!" Ben yells, pointing at a shrimp boat out in the sea.

"Me -thinks Blackbeard's Revenge sails upon these waters, Cap'n Benny." Fret says.

"Is he a mean pirate?" Ben asks Fret.

Ben grabs my shoulders and throws his arms around my neck, strangling me slightly in the process.

"Whoa, Cap'n. Loosen that grip a bit, eh?" I smile back at my cousin.

"Can we go out? I wanna see pirates!" Ben points to the shrimp boat again.

"C'mere, Cap'n." I swing Ben around so that he is now in my arms. "Let's see what a coupla old landlubbers can find out here."

"Y'all wait for me!"

Abby makes her way gingerly into the warm water. She appears to be grimacing with each step.

"Why's she making that face?" Fret asks me.

"I don't want to step on anything creepy or slimey. Oooo, oooo! What was that? Something darted across my foot! I'll never get to sing with Donny or Barry if a shark gets me now!"

Abby is playing this for all it is worth. She is funny.

"Don't you live here, Abby?" Fret asks. "You should be used to this stuff."

"Ooooo. Something ran across my foot. What was it y'all? Why are the critters only coming after me?"

She is jumping up and down, waving her arms up over her head.

"You are dancing around like a chicken with its head cut off, Abs. You are an absolute nut case!" I say while laughing and holding on tight to Ben.

"At least if I laugh so hard that I pee my pants, we're in the water." Abby says.

Even Ben giggles with us.

"There's another one! Crabs are made for boiling, not cruising around over my feet in the ocean." Abby says this in all seriousness.

"She is a looney tune if ever I saw one," Fret says flatly. He turns and dives into a wave.

"C'mon, Ben. Let's swim."

Abby yells at us to be careful.

Ben holds tight around my neck again as we venture deeper. I won't lie and say that I don't think about the sea creatures possibly lurking about on the sandy bottom, but the benefits far outweigh the risks in my mind.

"Look at the pelicans, buddy." I point out over the water to where a flock of twenty or so sits atop the moving sea.

"I love you, Sug." Ben kisses me on the cheek.

"Thanks, Ben." I kiss him back.

"And I love . . . pelicans." He blows them a kiss through the air without missing a beat. And again, we laugh.

Abby now stands next to us in the water.

"Here comes the Surfing Safari!"

Jay and the other boys come bounding into the water carrying inflatable rafts.

"Long time, no see," Blake says with a grin as he strongly pushes past us. "Hey, Ben," he adds.

"Hey!" Ben shouts back.

I don't know if he means to do it, but Blake's hand brushes my arm as he goes by. I feel a shiver and chill bumps.

Jay surfaces a little farther out, mounts his raft and paddles ahead of an incoming wave. He gives us a thumbs up as the wave carries him away.

Abby seems to now be completely happy and comfortable in the watery depths. Whitey helps her onto his raft and pulls her ahead of the breaking wave. He lets go at the right moment, and she squeals all the way to shore. Hank and David venture deeper to ride even bigger waves.

"I wanna ride!" Ben calls to no one in particular.

Jay comes over.

"C'mon, bud. Lay on your stomach. I'll jump on behind you when the wave comes."

Jay takes Ben from my arms.

I swim out to where Blake and Fret bob up and down, hanging onto Blake's raft. I grab an edge and float with them. As we kick, my leg brushes Blake's. A strange tingle again. I look at him. He looks at me. He felt it too. Fret is chattering away about pirates and Jaws, pelicans, and shrimp boats. Blake grins at me. I smile in return.

Now I'm embarrassed and decide to swim into shore.

Before I leave, I look at him again. I dive as gracefully as a dolphin away from the boys. I kick up my tanned legs behind me. I am sure my toes are perfectly pointed. The white of the bottom of my feet must make my legs appear even browner. I wonder if Blake notices these things.

He is a boy though. I'm sure that as soon as I took off, he turned his head back to the sea and Fret and Jaws, pirates, pelicans, and shrimp boats.

Chapter 24

E m, wake up if you're coming," Jay whispers, loudly.
"What time is it?" I groan and rub my eyes.

"Quarter to four. Whitey and Ret will be waiting. Get up now, or I'm going without you."

Lydia and Granddad are still sleeping as we leave the house in darkness. I follow Jay down to the dock.

The moon is almost full this morning, casting an eerie glow over the swollen river.

Jay has invited me along on the first fishing trip with his birthday present. Lydia and Granddad gave Jay this old Johnboat. It has a small motor with a handle on it, so we don't have to row.

Jay hands me the bucket of shrimp for bait. I breathe through my mouth and not my nose. I step down into the boat and set the bait in front of my seat. Jay pushes away from the pier and jumps in.

The air is still and feels slightly cool for a Carolina summer morning. I gaze back at the River Road home as Jay steers us out into the river. The front yard light twinkles in the darkness and bids a farewell. I think of Momma.

"This is a perfect birthday gift for you, Jay."

"Yeah."

"It's so quiet out here this early. Only a few birds screeching every now and then."

"Yes, Em. Let's keep it that way."

I take the hint. Jay does enjoy his quiet time. The hum of the boat motor almost lulls me to sleep after awhile. Jay navigates the dark waters like a native to this area. Granddad, Uncle Ty and Curtis taught him to fish on this river.

The sound of a grunting pig wakes me from my thoughts.

"Are there wild pigs in the woods?"

"There could be wild hogs, but that's a gator."

"In the river?" Now I'm alarmed.

"Too much salt out in the river. They do like the tributaries feeding into the river, the creeks and ponds. The noise just carries across the water, so it sounds like they're closer."

I can always count on Jay to know the answer to my questions about nature. He is always interested in both nature and cultures different from our own. Whenever we take a vacation, he's the first one to the tourist stand. He snatches up all the brochures. He reads them cover to cover and recites them back as if he's lived there all his life.

"There's Whitey and Ret." I motion in the direction of his friends.

They shine their flashlights in our eyes. Jay grabs the side of their boat to keep it from bumping against his own.

"Y'all sleep in this morning or what?"

"Shut up, White one. I had to pull your ass out of the sack," Retigan jokes.

"Watch the language while my sister's along. Okay, guys?"

"Why the hell, oops." Whitey covers his mouth in mock horror. "Now why is she along again?"

"I want her to see the old Guerreville site."

"That's where we're going, Jay?" I can't believe he is actually taking me out there. Again, I think of Momma and of the dream.

"Unless you'd rather go back," he challenges.

"Does the little baby sister need to go back and tell her granny?" Whitey says.

He and Retigan chuckle meanly.

"Jay knows I want to see the Guerreville site. I read about it last summer in a local history book, but we didn't have time to get out there." I remember that Momma had actually promised to take me this summer.

"Well, follow us, y'all. Stupid Yankees."

Whitey mutters the last part under his breath. Apparently not knowing or caring that the water carries sound. Retigan joins in the taunt.

"Ha! If it weren't for y'all damn Yanks raiding the place, it might still be there today!"

"Actually, Ret, didn't Mr. Guerre burn the place down?" I stupidly add.

Jay punches me in the back.

"Ow!" I glare at him.

"Let's just go, guys. We'll follow you."

Chapter 25

As we approach the point and the overgrown riverbank, the boys shine their flashlights on the shoreline. I see a partially exposed wall of bricks set back in the trees off the glint of one of the flashlights. The tide has gone out a bit. We take off our shoes and wade through the mud to get to shore.

"Watch the oyster shells, Em," Jay warns.

Whitey and Ret carry their boat onto the mud flat where it won't float away. Retigan doubles back to help Jay carry ours.

I step into the mud and feel an immediate warm contrast to the pre-dawn air. It is as if the heat of the daytime is all stored up inside that mud. I jump as a small crab scurries across my foot but keep my mouth shut, stifling a screech.

Jay and Ret set the boat on the shore. Jay turns and gives me an irritated look.

"Why'd you come along anyway, Em?"

Jay reaches down in the mud, grabs another crab and whips it right at my face.

"Boo!"

The boys snicker as I jump and let out a slight gasp. I choke back tears. Why did I come along this morning?

"She's just a little tit-less baby. Shouldn't even be out here. C'mon y'all. That is, anyone brave enough to come on." Whitey motions for us to follow.

I'm right on the heels of my brother. Wondering when he might act like a big brother and stick up for me.

Whitey has been given his name for a reason. His skin and hair are as white as a freshly laundered bed sheet. He wears his hair cropped short and spiked all over his head like a British punk rocker. He and Jay both like music imported from Great Britain. Retigan is Whitey's cousin from Charleston. He spends most of his summer with Ms. Jenkins and her boys. He is slight and shorter than Whitey with pale skin, dark hair and glasses.

"Are there snakes back in here, Jay?" I whisper, "I'm not scared, just wondering what I should be trying to avoid."

"There are snakes, Em, lots of them. But we're scaring them off left and right with all this racquet we're making."

Ret points his flashlight through the trees. "Looky here, y'all. Them foundations were once summer cottages. See that chimney over there?"

At first I can't see what he's talking about in the dark. Then through the Spanish moss hanging down, I begin to see shapes of burned-out chimneys here and there.

"Oh my goodness," I walk in the direction of the light. There are brick pieces lying around on the ground. It is definitely overgrown and mostly gone, but with its closeness to the river, I can see how a small summer community could have existed here before the Civil War.

"Em, look over here."

I push moss and branches out of my way and cross to where Jay stands. He flashes his light down towards something at his feet.

"Look at that."

I kneel down to get a better look.

"Maybe the rainy spring churned this ground up," Jay suggests.

He kneels down next to me. I pull what appears to be a small, iron cross out of the dirt, sand, and leaves.

"My flashlight just happened to catch it. I wonder if it's a Civil War relic."

"I don't know, Jay. Don't tell Whitey and Ret," I whisper.

The two other boys are behind a partial brick wall fishing something out of Ret's backpack. Jay and I exchange a knowing glance as Jay slips the cross into the pocket of his jeans.

"How about a smoke and a ghostly yarn from this old place?" asks Whitey.

"You go ahead. Emma and I will pass on the smoke."

"Of course, Yanks don't smoke," Whitey chortles. "Ret, you gonna tell this one?"

"Won't find this one in any old boring-ass history book, Em." Ret stares at me and Jay while Whitey lights his cigarette.

The lighter illuminates his glasses. He looks like a ghost himself. I shiver in spite of the increasingly warm air.

Jay reaches into his pocket. For a moment I think he's going to show them our find. Instead, he pulls out a piece of Juicy Fruit for the two of us to share.

"Yeah, Yankee soldiers settled over on Kiawah during the War between the States. They took over all that was there, but, of course, that weren't enough. Well, this here plot, Guerreville, was left abandoned as soon as the War began. Folks thought they'd be safer in Charleston. Truth be told, the Confederates ordered all locals out of St. John's Parish for their own safety," Ret begins.

"I've heard the Confederate soldiers wanted to live in many of the finer plantation homes while fighting the war," Jay adds.

"Yeah, yeah. Y'all are always trying to paint a picture, ain't ya? Anyhow, Guerreville was abandoned, but for a coupla slave gals and ol' Captain Guerre. Alfred Guerre was an old man with a fine home farther up along River Road. He refused to abandon the place. Some folks even speculated he had sympathetic leanings with his slaves, but he knew there'd be no place for him in local society with views like that.

"He'd ride a horse down here most evenings to check on the place. One night he noticed some boards missing from the outside of a couple houses and muddy footprints leading to the river. Well, he guessed right away that those Yankee soldiers was over here raiding his settlement. He could not stand by and watch his property be used to Northern advantage.

"Now, them slave ladies was hidden away pretty good, only coming out when the coast was clear. They was scared half to death of all the fighting and raiding going on around them. Maybe the Yanks knew they was hidden away there, but they left 'em alone. Old Cap'n Guerre probably didn't know they was there. The slave gals was afraid of him as much as they was afraid of the Union soldiers. It had long been rumored that Guerre was a crazy old man."

"Jeez, Ret. Tell them what happened already."

Whitey gives his cousin a pained look while flicking his cigarette butt into the trees.

"So, Cap'n Guerre waited till the next night. Soon as he saw them Union soldiers lighting out on their way across the Kiawah in their little make shift boats, he started setting those Guerreville cottages ablaze. Right in this spot where we sit. Well, those slave gals was holed up sleeping in one of them homes. The whole place was soon lit up. You might can imagine the scare old Guerre got when them gals come running outta one house, dresses blazing like the Fourth of July.

"Soon as the Yanks saw the fire, they stopped their rowing and watched. Guess they saw them two fiery figures come screaming down to the river bank. Story goes that the gals made it to the river alright but ain't one of 'em knew a lick about swimming. Damn Union soldiers tried to free two more slaves that night, but the gals was gone afore the Yanks could reach 'em. Supposedly, they buried their ashen remains over at Kiawah."

Ret stares into each of our faces and looks at the sky.

"Y'all hear that?"

"Must be a deer," Jay says.

"Or a panther," Whitey adds.

I give him a smirk, but I also hear the rustling. It sounds as if something is coming right at us through the woods.

"Why on earth would an animal be coming right toward us like that?" Jay says.

He moves a couple steps closer to me.

Whitey whispers and makes a circular motion with his hands. "Why don't y'all circle round one way. We'll go the other. See if we can spot it before it spots us,"

"Ya sure about that, Whitey?"

Retigan looks ready to make a run straight for the river.

"C'mon, Emma."

Jay pulls my shirt and heads deeper into the woods.

Chapter 26

J ay and I make our way through the dilapidated bricks and farther into the woods, away from the river.

"Looks like Whitey and Ret are going to the river."

"No. They're just circling wide, so we're sure to clear whatever's in the woods. It's a good idea. I'd like to spot it before it spots us."

Jay seems to believe his friends are actually sticking around.

"There isn't much to the old Guerreville site, is there? I thought it'd be a bit more interesting. More to see."

"Well, Em, it has been almost a hundred years ago. It was burned to the ground, and no one ever goes there."

"That's too bad. It's an interesting story. It could be some kind of historic landmark."

"I'm not sure the locals want tourists traipsing all over the area. It's bad enough in Charleston and at the beaches. That's probably what the locals think."

"Hear that, Jay? I hear the noise again. Which direction is it coming from?"

"Shhh. Hush up and listen."

The voice comes in low and loud, almost like a groan.

"Bessie, Bessie . . . I hear ya, Bessie. I canna see ya, Bessie."

"What on earth?" Jay quietly exclaims.

"Goodness. That's Mr. Tomson. I don't think Bessie is a cow."

"Look at the size of that gator!"

Jay and I peer through the dense underbrush into a clearing of marshy wetland. Mr. Tomson pushes awkwardly through the other side and sees the large and agitated alligator. The cavern where Mr.

Tomson's nose should be appears even more frightening in the dim light.

"Uh, Mr. Tomson, sir," Jay calls. "It's me, Jay Phend. Are you okay, sir?"

"There ya be, Bessie. Pipe down, big momma. I ain't gonna harm ye."

Mr. Tomson limps slowly in the direction of the gator. Bessie is perched on the edge of the swamp watching every move Mr. Tomson makes as he works his way closer. Her mouth is open wide exposing a set of large and scary teeth. A low moan seems to come from deep within her throat.

"Young man, I's just fine. Bessie here is angry though. She's got young 'uns tucked down in next to her. Y'all might wanna move on outta here."

Bessie looks like she's at least seven feet long. As we watch, she rises up on all four stubby, brownish legs and turns her mouth and eyes in our direction. The turn is slow, but Jay and I can tell from her strong-looking legs that she can probably move at a good clip.

"Look at her babies."

A creek cuts through the clearing into the swamp. Bessie's little ones are nestled into a mossy clump where the creek and swamp meet.

"Jay, let's go."

"You sure you're okay, Mr. Tomson, sir?"

"Enough already, Jay. Let's go." I hiss at my brother. "He's fine. He told us to leave."

"Get outta here, kids. Y'all don't wanna cross a gator defending her young. Might hafta mention to your grammy Lydia that y'all are out wandering before dawn. This is a fine lesson for y'all. Ya never know what's lurkin' in these parts."

Bessie takes two steps in our direction with her jaws open in a low, guttural moan. There is a thick stand of trees between us and her, but, finally, Jay's ready to leave. The gator lunges in our direction. We run for our lives!

I can't believe what we have just seen. I run at a dead sprint through the trees, anxious to get back to Jay's boat. I hear Jay running behind me.

"We've got to warn Whitey and Ret about the gators back in here!" Jay calls.

"Those jerks probably know about the gators. Where are they anyway?"

We run through a grove of trees thick as molasses, and I lead the way. Long branches and moss hang around us in all directions, shaking and swaying as we run. Looking up, I can see dappled sunlight starting to appear just in the very tops of the trees. It is still quite dark in these woods. I sweep aside branches as I run, careful not to hit Jay in the face. One branch seems to wrap around my hand.

"Aaaaaah! A snake!" I wave my arm with the snake attached. It flies off and smacks Jay squarely in the face.

"Aaaaah! Emma! I'm going to kill you!"

Jay runs ahead of me. I know he is scared too. I run next to him, trying to keep up.

"Wait! It was an accident. I'm sorry!"

"Let's just get the heck out of here!"

The Guerreville clearing and the water beyond are in sight. The sun coming up gives the river a grayish blue cast. Jay stumbles ahead of me. I trip on his foot, fall and take him down with me. We land hard in the sand and brush.

"I hate you, Em. I really do. I hate you."

"It was an accident, Jay. I'm sorry." I start to cry. I'm not sure why. Maybe from fright or my brother's harsh words. I realize Jay is crying too.

"I hate you. I hate everything. Why did Momma have to die? Why, Em? It's all so easy for you. You're Miss Happy-go-lucky, Miss Charmed Life. Everyone feels bad for poor little Emmy. What about me? She was my momma too. I loved her the most. I knew her the best. And now she's gone."

"I'm sorry, Jay. I didn't mean to hit you with the snake."

Jay wipes his eyes and leaves a smudge of mud across his face, mingled with tears.

"This isn't about the snake. You and Daddy and Fret . . . Fret's too little to understand. You and Dad just go on as if nothing's happened. I hate Dad. He was mean to her. Always fighting. Always arguing. He's glad she's gone. One less person to fight with."

We are both crying like a couple babies.

"They fought, but they loved each other too." My left arm is pinned under Jay. A burning pain is ripping through it. It feels like my arm is on fire. "Jay, I know you hate me right now, but I think my arm is broken."

"What?"

Jay looks down. He quickly pushes himself off the ground.

"It's fire ants! Get in the river quick!"

I push up after him. He swats at things I can't see as he runs to the water. He's slapping and clawing at his chest and head. If I wasn't in agony, I might laugh. I follow him to the river while scratching at the red swarm covering my left arm. Right after him, I plunge into the river.

"Shoot. Those sure are called fire ants for a reason. I thought my arm was broken. That really burns."

Jay doesn't speak as he ducks below the surface. He rubs his hands frantically across his head.

"They were all over my head. I didn't even realize. It's going to be hard to hide this trip from Lydia when we show up with bites all over us." He's still rubbing his head.

"I'm not hiding this outing from anyone." I look around thankful to see Jay's skiff right where he and Ret left it, but those darn boys are nowhere in sight. "Where'd your lovely best friends go?" I ask sarcastically.

"Well, Mr. Tomson and Bessie weren't part of the plan. Guess they were spooked and took off."

Jay and I are soaking wet as we idle away from shore. Jay is back to his usual quiet self except for the occasional fact he gives relating to nature. I'm not sure whether he wants to keep me informed or make me feel stupid. In movies and books, big brothers seem to look out for their little sisters.

The sun has come up enough now to change the gray cast to a promising orange and pink sky over the eastern end of Kiawah. I cry again at this breathtaking sight. The moon appears to be setting at the other end of the river. Have I ever seen a moonset?

"Please don't hate me, Jay. I've been thinking you and Daddy are the ones who've forgotten about Momma . . . you go on as if she never existed." The tears drop onto my wet shirt blending with the salty river water.

Jay has tears in his eyes.

"It's not your fault, Em. I know that. I was just being a baby back there. Dad expects me to be a man. I miss Momma so much."

"I do too."

He pats my shoulder and smiles weakly.

"Your arm alright?"

"Soon as I got those devilish little beasts off, it felt better."

"Here. You keep this. Maybe Lydia knows what it is."

Jay pulls the iron cross from his pocket and hands it to me. I take the relic and run my hand across its smooth surface.

"Ya know, Jay, I could have sworn Bessie was a cow."

Chapter 27

The room is dark. White forms looking like horse saddles lurk in the shadows. My heart beats quickly in my chest. My palms sweat.

What is this place?

A white form moves and moans in the corner.

Clouds release the moon from their shadow outside the window. A dim light enters the room. The figure in white rolls over to face me. The eyes do not appear to see me.

What I thought was one figure is actually two. Four eyes peer through me in the darkness. I smell the smoke and hear the shouting at the same time.

I try to yell to the dark figures . . . *run! Escape while you can!*

The words do not leave my frozen lips.

The figures rise and run through me to the window. They are young black girls. They look alike and close in age. I move to the window with them. They still do not notice me.

Their faces are masks of pure terror. They peer out the window. I lean over too and see flames shooting from the door below.

No Damn Yanks will have my property! Damn them to hell!

An old man (looking curiously like Mr. Tomson) runs clumsily with a flaming torch.

The girls leave the room. They stumble and seem to be confused. They are very thin. Maybe they are hungry. I want to help them. I cannot move from my post by the window.

I see the girls run from the doorway below. Orange flames leap from them, turning their white dresses to black ash. Their screams fill the night air.

The old man sees them. He turns to run and falls with the torch. Flames spread across the ground quickly.

My left arm burns. Again I try to scream.

Chapter 28

I open my eyes to see Lydia staring at me. Kona barks in the back yard. I hear the playful shouts of my brothers as well. Lydia, however, is not looking very playful.

"What are the boys doing?" Maybe it's something interesting enough to take me away from this stare.

"Your Uncle Ty and Curtis are helping them erect that soccer goal your daddy sent."

Lydia lights a cigarette and stares past me.

"Were you having a bad dream?" She asks.

"What? Oh, I guess so."

"Would you like to talk about it?"

"Not really."

"Sug . . ."

Lydia looks at me. I can see the concern in her eyes.

"I've been having strange dreams the whole time we've been here. At home, I had sweet dreams of Momma. I didn't want to wake up. I would try to go back to sleep, so we could be together again. Now, here, my dreams are just down right creepy."

"You seemed upset just now while you were sleeping there on the settee. What happened on the fishing trip this morning? Anything interesting?"

Oh, that's it. She knows something. That's why she looked angry when I woke up.

"Didn't Jay tell you all about it?" I'm hoping.

"Jay didn't say a word. That's why I'm asking you. In fact, I just received a phone call from Ms. Dexter. Do you know who that might be, Emma?"

"That Mr. Tomson's daughter?"

"It sure is, and why do you suppose she'd be calling me this morning?"

"Mr. Tomson's alright, isn't he?"

"He is, but Ms. Dexter said he was mumbling something fierce about you children being out with Bessie and her baby gators. Out near the old Guerreville site."

Lydia's looking straight through me now with that "go to heck" eyebrow cocked as high as I've ever seen it.

"Really, Lydia. It was those rude boys, Whitey and Retigan. Well, Jay did want to show me the old site. I've always wanted to see it. Momma promised to take me this summer. But those boys turned everything into something mean. They left us out there. Lydia, I was scared. I think Jay was too. Then we saw Mr. Tomson with the gators. Did you know Bessie was a big momma gator? I thought she was a cow. She has baby gators too." I'm telling the story and making excuses a mile a minute.

"I'm certainly happy that y'all are back here safely after your harrowing ordeal."

I detect just a hint of sarcasm.

"However, Emma, child, do you realize that your daddy would not let y'all come stay here if he didn't trust me and Granddad?"

"Yes, ma'am."

"Well, what do you suppose your daddy would think of the two of you sneaking off? Telling us you were fishing when instead y'all decide to go out Guerreville way?"

"He wouldn't like it one bit. Jay's probably caught the flat end of a wooden spoon for a whole lot less." I look seriously over at Lydia.

"The woods and cricks around here aren't like those in Indiana. Yes, you saw the gators, but there are also snakes, spiders, even bobcats out there. Things that seem funny can turn dangerous in a heartbeat."

Lydia again stares out at the river as if thinking about scenes pulled from her bank of memories.

"Lydia, I won't do it again."

"I'm not trying to discourage exploration, but we have to know what you children are up to . . . at all times."

I itch my arm distractedly. Lydia notices.

"What happened there, Sug?"

She points at my arm, and I look down to see the small red welts covering it.

"Fire ants got us. Jay and I had to jump in the river to get them off of us."

"Sounds like the two of you were behaving like a couple of fools this morning. I'm quite disappointed in Jay for getting you both into such a situation. He really should know better."

"He knew how badly I've always wanted to see the Guerreville site. It wasn't his fault those darn boys left us out there."

"We'll be having a word soon as there's a quiet moment. Those two sure are excited about that soccer goal, huh?"

"Yeah. I've never seen Uncle Ty and Curtis so excited." I grin in her direction.

"Sug! You know I'm talking about your brothers," Lydia smiles. "You doing alright?"

Now it's my turn to gaze out to the river.

"Back home, I couldn't help thinking about Momma most of the time and feeling sorry for myself a lot. But since we've been here, sometimes I go a whole stretch of time without thinking about her. Then I feel guilty. I'm selfish because sometimes I want to forget. I want to pretend it never happened. I want to feel the carefree way I used to feel. Really, I can't even remember how that felt. The feeling that your parents would always be there when you wake up in the morning. Momma always had her tea, but she made coffee for Daddy. He doesn't even drink coffee any more. I guess because she's not there to make it for him. Every once in a while, she'd surprise us with fresh-baked cookies after school. She was in such a good mood on those days, and the house smelled amazing. Life seemed so happy then. Simple things . . . but that's what I miss the most."

"My dear sweet Sugar . . ."

Lydia sits next to me on the settee and takes me gently into her strong embrace. This woman is a puzzle to me. She is all strength and iron fist, yet gentle and velvet gloved at the same time. I snuggle into her side and smell smoke, green grass and Chanel no. 5. I take a deep breath in and let it out slow and jagged.

"I know you miss her as much as I do Lydia." I look up into her face to see a tear trickling down her worn and sun-kissed cheek.

"In a way that I hope you will never know, Sug. I raised that sweet girl as my own. There's nothing easy in burying your child. Just as every child needs a mother. We don't know why the good Lord takes one and leaves another. I try not to be hateful, but I do have my thoughts about that gal who took her from us."

"What do you mean, Lydia?" Really, I don't know.

"The gal who hit your momma head-on. Eighteen years old and drunk out of her mind. Lost her teeth in the collision and was more concerned about that than the fact that she killed someone."

Lydia's tear is gone. She is angry with these thoughts.

"I hadn't really thought about the person who killed Momma . . . only that she's gone. I'd like to call her up and give her a piece of my mind. Idiot." I join Lydia in anger.

Lydia's anger goes as quickly as it arrived. She pulls me close again, kissing my forehead.

"Sug, I'm sorry. I should not have shared that with you. I can't help but feel angry at times."

She's quiet for a moment. Shouts and laughter are in the air. It sounds like more kids have joined my brothers in a heated soccer match.

"Anger is not an emotion that does one any good. Don't be angry, Sug. That poor gal will suffer more than we will ever know because of this. Our anger over the matter won't bring your mother back."

The breeze seems to pick up over the river shaking the Spanish moss in the trees and gently bending the old Oak down by the river's edge. Lydia and I tilt our heads back and close our eyes at the same time, accepting the breeze as a brief gift in the humid morning. As we sit quietly, I feel a poke in my left hip.

I reach into the pocket of my jean shorts and pull out the rusty relic. Lydia glances over and takes it from my hands.

"Where on earth did y'all find this?"

She turns the odd cross-shaped object over in her hands. She runs her fingers along the thing as if it were a precious gem.

"I've not seen such a thing in ages. Takes me back."

"Jay and I found it this morning at Guerreville. What is it?"

"I'll be damned."

Lydia continues to stare at the object. A smile works its way into the corners of her mouth.

"What is it, Lydia?"

"It's an old tool, Sugar. Goodness, my daddy used to have these lying around his mechanic's shop. My daddy was an auto mechanic, but before that he repaired buggies, wagons and even shoed horses. He was generally handy and interested in anything that could run faster than a man." She smiles to herself and chuckles. "During prohibition, Daddy was known to have the fastest cars around. We all took turns running liquor from the mountains to the coast and back again. He was never a big drinker himself but thought prohibition was Puritanical and plum-crazy. Plus, his momma (my grandmother) was French, and she couldn't get along without her wine. Some said she made the best Beef Bourguignonne this side of the Atlantic. She taught me how to cook right here in this kitchen."

"So what sort of tool is that, Lydia?" She's gotten off the subject a bit here.

"Well, it would have been a common tool back in the late 1800s. When Guerreville thrived, folks needed to care for their horses hooves. It is a tool that was used to bear up horseshoes."

"What do you mean? I thought that had to do with making coffee . . . strong enough, ya know?"

"Sug, you are a peach. Oh my. This little tool was placed into the horseshoe. The end was pounded in order to 'bear up' or apply the horseshoe. Not many ladies were strong enough, but my grandmother was. My daddy always joked that his momma made coffee that was also strong enough to 'bear up a horseshoe.' We were raised on the stuff, and the phrase stuck, I guess."

Lydia hands me the relic.

"Interesting that it's shaped like a cross, Lydia."

"Mighty interesting, Sug. You hang on to that."

Chapter 29

I run around back to see what the boys are doing. Uncle Ty and Curtis have erected the soccer goal and placed it at the end of a grassy area, away from the garden. They appear to be full participants in the soccer match. It looks like they are using rules similar to half-court basketball, another favorite past-time of my brothers.

I sit on the veranda to watch the game hoping someone might notice me eventually and invite me to play. There are bikes parked in the driveway. Jay and Uncle Ty are teamed up with Retigan, David and Blake while Curtis and Fret play with Hank and Whitey. Curtis spots me first.

"Hey there, Emma. Come on and join us. We need another player on our team."

"Don't have to ask me twice!"

I jump from the top step to the ground and avoid looking at Whitey and Ret. Hopefully they are behaving in a civil manner since the adults are playing. Fret gives me a high five as I pass, and Blake smiles in my direction. Kona sits near the goal, ready to assist with defense whenever possible. They're skins, and we're shirts.

"You take the ball out, Em."

Curtis then comes close enough to whisper.

"I'm going to break right. Fret's going to cut left towards the goal. You pass it out wide to me, and I'll get it to Fret. Got it?"

"Got it."

I look to the left where Hank and Whitey jockey for position in front of Jay and Blake. David hangs back near Fret, and Uncle Tyson hovers near the goal. I have to get it by Retigan to get it to Curtis. While still looking left in a fake, I plant my right foot and kick the ball as hard as I can with my left foot in a decent pass to Curtis breaking right. He executes a perfect one touch pass to Fret who is breaking left and to the goal. Fret dribbles right around both David and Uncle Ty and takes a big boot at the goal.

"He scores again! Oh yeah, uh huh."

Fret bops around doing his little victory dance. The guys on the opposing team shake their heads.

"Now that was just too easy. We only let you get that one by us, so Emma could gain some confidence," Jay states.

"Looks like Fret's the confident one," I reply.

We all laugh while Fret continues his victory dance, flashing a gaping, toothless grin.

"Mr. Hann, we're going for a bike ride soon, right?" asks Blake.

"Call me, Curtis, son, and yes. That's the rumor I've been hearing."

Just then Lydia comes out on the veranda with watermelon slices and a jug of sweet tea. We scatter from the soccer match to get in on the snack.

"Alright, y'all. I'll have lunch ready for you back here after your ride."

"Thank you kindly, Lydia, but I'll have to get back to work as soon as we're done riding. I'll be staying out on the island," Curtis says.

"I need to get back now, Lydia, but thanks."

Uncle Ty plants a kiss on Lydia's cheek while munching a piece of watermelon. She wipes the juice off her face and swats her grandson's arm.

"I think that palmetto bug is trying to get some watermelon."

Fret points toward a very large bug scurrying across the veranda.

"He won't eat much," Uncle Ty says.

"Well, let's go guys. Nature awaits!" Fret calls.

Chapter 30

W hitey, David and Retigan decide against the bike ride, but Jay, Fret, Hank, Blake, and I are right behind Curtis. We follow the narrow dirt path through the pine and palmetto forest towards the marsh. Curtis must look a lot like his dad because I don't see much of Ms. Hat in him. She is tiny, brown and frail-looking, but Curtis is tall, broad-shouldered and very dark brown. He and Marcy make quite a picture when they are together. Her paleness against his darkness shows that opposites do attract. He stops every so often to point out items of interest.

"Did Indians really live on this island, Curtis?" Fret asks.

"Heck, yeah, Fretty. They were here long before history was even recorded. A small tribe called the Kiawah was here when the first white settlers arrived. The Ashepoo, the Edistos, the Wandos, they all lived in tiny coastal villages."

"What kind of houses did they have?" I ask.

"See the palmetto leaves here, Sug?"

We all nod our heads.

"They used these to build small, round huts. Did you notice that the tribes I named are now names of rivers?"

"Yes! Granddad told me that the rivers are named after the Indian tribes who lived here," Jay says. "Granddad Travis is a descendant of the Ute Indians of northwest Colorado."

"That's right, Jay." Curtis turns his dark eyes away from us and to the marsh. "The tribes were separate, small tribes because of those natural barriers. The rivers, the ocean, the marshes kept them apart, on separate islands. Follow me, y'all. I'll show you something really cool."

He takes a path back onto the main road. We follow the road for awhile, past homes and a golf course being built, to a stretch of dirt road crossing a large pond.

"Watch the gator!" Fret yells.

There is a large alligator sunning itself on the grass between the road and the pond.

"Do you think that's Bessie?" I ask Jay giving him a sideways glance.

"No, Emma," he laughs. "The currents are too strong in the river for Bessie to want to get out in that open water. Maybe that's her sister."

"The gators round here are probably like the Indians used to be . . . tribes separated by water." Hank adds.

"Who's Bessie?" Fret asks, "I thought that was Mr. Tomson's cow."

"We'll explain later, Fret," I tell him.

Curtis stops his bike in the middle of the road and stretches his arm in a sweeping motion across the scene in front of us.

"Look here, y'all. Enjoy this natural view while you can. If they listen to me at all, this will be done the right way. But this land ahead of us is called Rhett's Bluff. The Turks are planning a small housing development on the land."

"Are they nice, Curtis? The developers?" I ask.

"Oh, shoot yeah. They're trying to make a buck, like anyone, and they hired me, didn't they?" He says with a grin. "Lydia and your Uncle Ty helped bring them in here. They can't be too bad."

"They did?" Jay asks.

"Well, some folks were scared to death of foreigners buying this island, but Lydia and Travis have been close to Dr. Kaseem for years. His nephew, Umit, is one of the investors. You've met him, right kids?"

"Yes. Umit was a member of Turkey's National Football Club. He's met Pele!"

Jay exclaims.

"That's right. Well, he's the one who brought his fellow countrymen in on this deal."

"So what are they going to do with Rhett's Bluff?" Hank asks.

"C'mon y'all. Let me show you."

"Look at that gator now," Blake says.

We turn to look back where the gator was, but now he's gliding slowly through the water, close to the road, keeping an eye on us.

"She might have a little one nearby," Blake says.

"You're probably right," Curtis adds.

The land ahead of us does appear to be a bluff in that it sits higher than the land around it. It looks like an island but really is more of a peninsula. I realize this as I examine the spit of ground we are riding out on. It looks like a natural bridge between the pond on our right and an opening to the river on our left.

As we reach the bluff, it looks like the road we are on circles around the area, veering to the right and left. Curtis rides to the left and motions for us to stop.

"Look at this."

He gets off his bike and walks over to a built up area leading into a thick band of pine and oak trees.

"What do y'all think this is?" Curtis asks us.

"Looks like an oyster bed," Fret says.

"That is what it looks like on first glance. See, the developers are going to incorporate this into the landscape of whatever home goes in here."

"Why are they doing that?" Hank asks.

"Have y'all ever heard of a midden?"

We mutter "no" and shake our heads.

"It's quite miraculous really that it's still here. A midden is an ancient trash pile."

"O . . . kay," says Fret, wanting more exciting information, obviously.

"Well, on first glance it just looks like a bunch of oysters stuck in dirt. But, I had some of my geologist friends come down here from USC and the way the oyster shells are arranged indicates a dumping ground. There are also pieces of clay dishes in there. Dishes used by the Indians."

"That's pretty cool, Mr. Hann." Blake says.

"Mr. Hann at school, Blake, but you can call me Curtis out here. We think this midden dates back to 1500 B.C. and is one of the only traces of the indigenous people."

"How long were the Indians here on Kiawah?" Jay asks.

"By the late 1600s they'd been persuaded to give up most of their lands in exchange for cloth, hatchets and other needed items. By the 1740s they had completely disappeared. The plantation owners had come along by then, and that's something else I'd like to show y'all out here on the bluff."

We follow Curtis around the dirt road to the left. The trees and brush are thick, but I catch an occasional glimpse of the marsh and river through the trees.

"Leave your bikes here."

A narrow path can be seen through the woods. Curtis, looking quite serious, motions for us to follow. Hank and my brothers are right behind him, but Blake stops to hold a branch back for me to pass.

"This is really cool," he whispers. "Thanks for letting me come along."

"You're so lucky to live here," I tell him.

"Maybe someday you'll live here too."

"Maybe," I reply as we catch up with the others.

"Look, y'all."

Curtis points through the trees. For some reason I notice how white his nails look against the deep brown of his skin. I see where he's pointing. There is a broken down brick chimney with more brownish-red bricks scattered around on the ground.

"This was the location of one of the first plantation homes on the island. Right here where we stand. It was situated back here on the river to take advantage of the travel routes. It was easier for folks to travel by water than on land."

"So a house stood right here?" Fret asks.

"Yeah, Fretty. Follow me."

We continue along the path into a clearing with a circular dirt drive, a boat launch and a gazebo near the river's edge.

"I wish the plantation home was still here," I say.

"That would be something, Emma. Most likely it was destroyed by fire during the Civil War," Curtis says.

He stops to point out a leafy plant with small red blossoms.

"We think these cannas were part of the landscape of that home. They can't be found anywhere else on the island and are quite unusual for this area."

"Who set the place on fire?" Hank asks.

"The Union soldiers occupied Kiawah, right Curtis?" Jay adds.

"They did later, that's right. But they probably didn't burn it down. They could have used it for shelter. In fact, the other home on the island at the time still stands. Union soldiers actually left messages on the walls. We're not sure why one was left alone and the other burned."

"It ties in with the Guerreville story, right Emma?" Jay says. "They could have crossed the river right here to get over there."

Jay points across the river. My breath is almost taken away by the beauty of the view. The river is wide and deep in this spot, and I can imagine using the river to travel to and from Charleston or to visit relatives and friends on other islands. But as I look across to the point where the Kiawah and Stono Rivers meet, I don't care to think about going back to Guerreville. Blake taps my shoulder and points out a lone heron flying low over the glistening water. Fret runs off chasing a fiddler crab down onto the muddy riverbank.

Chapter 31

I thought the weekend would never get here." I say this to Abby as she climbs out of her momma's old station wagon.

"Y'all have a good time now, ya hear?" Mrs. Doyle calls, "See you at mass Sunday morning."

She begins to drive away, and Abby and I hug briefly before waving good-bye to Mrs. Doyle.

"It's absolutely hotter than Hades, Em. That alone has made this week drag on forever." Abby wipes the sweat from her brow. "How are we getting out to Blake's anyway?"

"Uncle Ty is running us over in the pontoon boat. I'm not sure about playing tennis with all the experts down here."

"Well, Blake said his older sister would play with us. She's on the high school team, and she's been teaching kids out at Kiawah this summer." Abby explains.

"It'll be fun, I guess. Hopefully my brothers won't do anything too embarrassing."

Arm in arm, we walk around to the riverfront to wait for my uncle. We sit on the end of the pier and dangle our feet into the cool river water.

"Time really does fly when I'm here, Abs. I only have a couple weeks left, and my dad will be here next weekend." I move my feet slowly back and forth through the blue-green water.

"Next weekend! You can't leave that soon. It seems like you just got here."

"We're not leaving then. That's just when Daddy gets here. Usually he stays a week or so before we go home."

"Oh, good, but I still don't want you to go."

Abby gently knocks her pale foot against my brown one in the water.

"We'll have to make the most of the time that's left . . . starting today!"

I put my arm around her shoulder. We rock side to side, laughing and kicking the water high in the air. A pelican squawks at us and glides away after we rudely interrupt his morning nap.

* * *

I like Blake's sister, Deena, as soon as I see her on the tennis court. She's not real tall, but lean, so she probably looks taller than she is. She's wearing a white, pleated tennis skirt with a pale yellow t-shirt and a light blue and yellow argyle sweater vest. Her long, straight, brown hair is pulled back in a low ponytail revealing one of the kindest-looking faces I have ever seen. Have you seen a face like that? Ordinary, really, but something about it makes you feel like Jesus Christ lives behind those eyes. As much as Blake's eyes are that amazing turquoise blue and almond shaped, Deena's eyes are deep brown and round. Her smile is wide and gentle as she turns to greet me and Abby.

"Hey, y'all," she says slowly. She confidently extends a hand to me. "I'm Deena Feegan, and you must be the infamous Emma Phend." She laughs gently and winks at Abby.

As I shake Deena's hand, she pulls me into a hug.

"Emma, I don't know you yet, but I like the looks of you already. My little brother can't stop talking about you. Emma this and Emma that. And, girl," she whispers in my ear. "I'm so sorry 'bout your momma."

I'm embarrassed but try to show her with my smile that her kindness is appreciated.

"Well, little bro,' I'd say you have excellent taste in friends." She emphasizes the word friends for dramatic effect.

It is Blake's turn to be embarrassed. He has turned a couple deeper shades of red, but everyone laughs and the awkward moment is soon forgotten.

"Who is this little cutie-pie?" Deena turns her attention to Fret.

Blake chimes in, "This is Emma's little brother, Fret, and you already know Jay."

"Yes, hey, Jay. Fret, it is very nice to make your acquaintance." Deena extends her hand to Fret but also pulls him into an embrace.

"Can we play tennis now?" Fret asks.

"Of course! Abby, Emma and Fret can come with me. Hank, you, Blake and Jay can play on court two."

"Is this okay with Coach Clay?" Hank asks Deena.

"As long as we groom the courts when we're done."

"We'll put little runner girl on that task," Hank jokes. "She has the endurance for the job."

"Nice, Hank. What is he talking about?" Deena asks us.

"Oh, he saw me running one day." I shake my head. "You'll help me groom the courts, right?"

"He's just kidding, Emma. We'll all pitch in."

Deena gives us instruction in the game of tennis and feeds us balls for an hour or so. I think I could really like tennis. Fret has wandered off to look for snakes, lizards, and bugs in the wooded area surrounding the tennis courts. Hank and Jay are playing singles, so Blake joins us on our court.

"How 'bout a doubles match?" Blake asks.

"Me and Abby against you and Emma?" Deena questions.

"An actual match?" I'm not sure. "I can't serve very well."

"Neither can Abby, and she's been taking lessons all summer," Blake teases.

"Blake Feegan, you shut your trap." Abby sticks out her tongue at Blake with a pouting look.

This irritates me slightly.

"It's a joke! C'mon, Em. I'll help you. Besides, we're just having fun," Blake says.

"You serve first. Fret, are you okay out there?" I call.

"Fine, Em. Just on wildlife patrol."

"That would be my concern exactly."

We play doubles, making shots, missing shots, and laughing a lot. Jay and Hank finish their match and cheer us from the wooden bleacher steps next to the court.

"Is Coach Clay really dating Ms. Jenkins?" Abby asks the Feegans during a water break.

"Shh . . . he's inside, Abby." Hank holds his finger up to his lips. "I don't doubt it. He's a skirt chaser from what I hear anyway. I've heard he lost a big match in college because of it."

"She wore sunglasses all week at cheer practice after the Fourth. The girls were saying her ex hit her because he saw her with Coach Clay," Abby says.

"Don't understand that line of thinking. What guy is going to hit a girl? That's not right." Blake looks at his older sister who's glaring at him. "You don't count!"

"That was hilarious anyway. Blake once hit me in the teeth. Teeth full of braces, mind you, so he scratched his knuckles up something good. I was so mad that I threw the box of Bisquick I was holding right at him . . . hit him squarely between the eyes. He scared me to death because then he screamed and pretended to be blind. I felt horrible, but he was totally faking."

Deena punches Blake playfully on the arm.

"Anyway, I think Coach felt horrible about what happened to Ms. Jenkins because of him," Deena adds.

I listen to them quietly. Abby is hanging on every word.

"How on earth did Coach Clay lose a big college match because he's a skirt-chaser?" she asks.

"I heard it from some of the other coaches." Hank begins. "Apparently, Coach played for Clemson, and of course, they have a big rivalry with S.C. The S.C. guys knew Coach Clay pretty well, knew his reputation anyway. He was in a tight match at one singles with their top player, conference championship on the line.

"The S.C. guys strategically placed the beautiful kid sister of one of their players front and center on Coach's court. The guys were going to a third set tiebreaker for the championship. Well, this girl started rooting for Coach Clay loud enough for him to take note of her. Let's just say Coach Clay lost a bit of his tennis focus.

"It's not usually a good idea in the middle of a long rally to start thinking about the pose you're striking as you lunge for the ball. It's even rumored that Coach Clay glanced over in the middle of his service motion to see if she was watching him.

"Coach lost that tiebreak seven to zero, and his team lost the conference title. He apparently said the loss would have been worth it had he been able to find that girl after the match. She mysteriously disappeared as soon as the tie-break ended." Hank finishes.

"Sounds like cheating to me." Deena says.

The girls agree, and the boys just laugh. Just then, Fret comes running around the back side of the small tennis center building.

"Hey! I was chasing a lizard over there and guess what I saw?"

Fret is hopping from foot to foot as if he has to pee.

"A bobcat?" Deena guesses.

"A rattler?" Jay adds.

"What is it, Fret?" Blake asks.

"It's the tennis guy and Ms. Claudette. I think they're wrestling on the floor in there." Fret points to the tennis building.

"Speak of the devil," says Abby.

"You're kidding me! C'mon, y'all." Hank waves at us to follow.

"He was biting at her and she was clawing at him. Her nails are like daggers!" Fret is beside himself. "Is she alright? I thought Coach was nice when I met him."

"You stay here, Fret," Jay says. "Hank and I will check and make sure everything is alright."

Jay and Hank go off smirking and slinking around the building. Blake looks like he's not sure what to do here. His sister is looking at him disapprovingly, but he appears more afraid of facing his brother's taunts for not going along.

"Wait for me!" Blake calls quietly after the boys.

"Oh, I cannot miss out on this." Abby chases after him.

Deena, Fret and I sit on the bleachers to wait for them. Probably if Fret hadn't been along and so upset, I would have been spying with them.

After a short while, the boys and Abby come around the corner of the building. At the same time, Ms. Claudette comes out the front door of the tennis center. She glances down where we sit.

"Oh, hey, y'all," She calls in her sing-song drawl. "Pleasant afternoon we're having, ain't it?"

"Yes, ma'am," we call.

Deena and I cover our mouths to keep the giggles from escaping.

"You alright, Ms. Claudette?" Fret asks.

Deena and I clamp our hands over his mouth. I tell him to keep quiet with my eyes.

"What's that, Fretty?" Ms. Claudette asks while straightening her tennis skirt.

"He was talking to the other boys," Deena calls.

They wave up to Ms. Jenkins. She shrugs her shoulders, waves a general good-bye, and moves up the path through the woods to her car.

"Is everything okay?" Fret asks again.

"Wooo. Everything is just fine, Fret. I'm sure of it. Nothing to be worried about," Hank begins. "I think Ms. Jenkins and Coach were just going over tennis strategy."

"Fighting like that?" Fret asks.

"Sometimes tennis can be a very physical game. I'm sure he was just showing her how to protect herself." Jay holds his sides, bent over, laughing.

"You're crazy," Fret says to Jay. "And I'm hungry."

"Let's clean up here then, and get on over to the house," Deena says. "Our parents are expecting us."

As we all begin clean-up work, Coach Clay exits the tennis shop. He sees us and looks slightly uncomfortable.

"Good evening, y'all," he says. "How was the match?"

"Great, Coach. Thank you," replies Deena.

"I'll see y'all later at your parent's party." Coach waves with one hand while spraying *Binaca* in his mouth with the other.

Chapter 32

T he Feegan family is originally from Louisville, Kentucky. Abby
told me that they were frequent visitors to the Low country and
decided to move down here permanently. Mr. Feegan came down first
to talk to the island developers. He got to know Curtis and my uncle
while he was here. Curtis advised on protecting the natural habitat
around their home site, and Uncle Ty helped build the house. Their
home sits in a new little neighborhood on the river side of the island,
not too far from the tennis courts and close to the golf course, as well.

I heard Uncle Ty and Curtis talking the other evening about how
much they admire Buck Feegan. A self-made man, they called him.
They said he grew up dirt poor with one school uniform to wear every
day of the week. He was the only Irish kid in his Italian Catholic school
back in Kentucky. When he first went to the school, he was beat up
every day on his way home. Not only did he have only one school
uniform, but that uniform had knickers when the rest of the school wore
long pants. His momma would stay up late every school night
laundering and mending his uniform. Finally, a strong Italian girl
befriended him, walked him home each day, and the beatings ended.

According to Curtis and Uncle Ty, Buck Feegan was the first in his
family to go to college. He married his high school sweetheart, Mrs.
Feegan, became a marine, and eventually owned his own business.
They said Mr. Feegan is an eternal optimist with a zest for life that
cannot be defeated.

As we approach the front door of the Feegan home, it sounds like
there is a party in full swing. The sun is setting, so the outdoor lights on
the wide veranda welcome us. Up the stairs, large wicker couches and
coffee tables are placed along either side of the inviting entry. Beautiful

baskets filled with blue hydrangeas rest on each of the tables. The blue of the flowers ties in perfectly with the creamy pale yellow color of the house. It sounds like a band is warming up on the river side.

"Is a band playing tonight, Blake?" I ask.

"Oh, yeah. It's my brother and sister's band."

"Hank and Deena are in a band?" Fret asks.

"No. It's Gabe and Melanie. They're in college," Blake replies. "They'll play oldies to keep the parents happy, but they'll play some cool new music too."

"If you know anything at all about Blake, it is that he adores music. I don't know how he does it, but he'll find music from England that no one has even heard. Our brother, Gabe, loves that stuff," Deena adds.

"I believe it's called Radio Europe on National Public Radio, Sunday nights," Hank says.

"I love good music too. I listen to that program when I can. I had a band at home for a little while, but we've disbanded," Jay says in mock seriousness. "It's depressing, really."

"Maybe because your songs were the stupidest things anyone has ever heard," I say. "I've gotta take a squirt and it's starting to hurt. Come on!"

The other kids laugh.

"My chick treats me like a prick . . . and that's what makes me totally sick!" Fret sings.

"That was a song they sang?" Hank asks.

"C'mon, I wrote that one. Very serious stuff here . . . meant to soothe the soul."

"Only if laughter's the best medicine," Deena teases.

I can tell Jay enjoys Deena's attention.

"Hey that's the title of a book. Lydia has that one," Jay says.

"Erma Bombeck, Jay," I tell him.

"I'm starving!" Fret announces again. "I sure hope y'all have some good grub in this purty house." Fret exaggerates a southern drawl.

We all laugh again and follow the Feegans inside.

Lydia and Ms. Hat are standing in the spacious kitchen chatting with an attractive couple. I assume they are Mr. and Mrs. Feegan. They all turn to watch us as we make our way into the kitchen.

"Hello there," Mrs. Feegan smiles warmly at us.

"Hi, Mom. You know Abby. This is Jay and Emma, and this cutie-pie is Fret." Deena points to each of us in turn.

"It is certainly my pleasure to meet you all. I'm Mrs. Feegan, and this handsome devil by my side here is Mr. Feegan."

He comes around the kitchen island, shakes Jay's hand, winks at Abby, and proceeds to pick Fret and me up into a big bear hug.

"You kids run on out and grab some dinner. You must be starving after your tennis match. Blake, did you get a chance to practice your toss at all?"

Mr. Feegan smiles, but I can tell he's serious about his son getting his practice in before playing with us.

"Sure, Dad. Hold it like a can of soda. Toss out front and to the right, just like you told me," Blake replies. "Thanks for the tip."

My brothers and I hug Lydia and Ms. Hat as we pass. I can hear the Feegans commenting on the "lovely children" as we cross into the front yard. I am happy to see an in-ground swimming pool on the river-side of their home. The reflection of the darkening sky and the interior pool lights give the water a shimmering purple glow. A small tent is set up on the patio next to the pool with a table and covered dishes. There are older teenagers and adults chatting in groups around the pool and yard. Many face the band, waiting for the music to begin.

Deena pours me a lemonade while I make a plate of barbecued shrimp skewers, mini-crab cakes and potato salad. The band begins to play a Beach Boys tune. It looks like many of the adults have been enjoying Mrs. Feegan's sangria recipe because they are already dancing like a bunch of fools.

Uncle Ty, Aunt Katy and Ben dance in a circle with Marcy and Curtis. Ben sees me watching them and waves. I wave and smile in return. Uncle Ty says something to them that I can't hear and hurries into the house. Lydia, Granddad and Ms. Hattie sit on the river-side veranda with the Feegans and some other guests.

Abby and I hit each other and giggle as we notice Coach Clay and Ms. Claudette dancing near the edge of the pool. After seeing Ms. Claudette looking so miserable the one day at the beach house, it's nice to see her smiling. Fret, Jay, Blake, Whitey, Hank and David Alan race around the yard with squirt guns in hand.

"Blake, Blake."

This must be his sister, Melanie, calling from the band. She looks like a cross between Deena and Blake. She has long blond hair and the round brown eyes.

"This next song is for Blake. This is a new band from overseas. This song has just been released in the States, and the band is called the Police."

The boys stop chasing around like idiots and listen as the guy who looks like a darker-haired Blake steps up to the mike. All is quiet in anticipation of what Gabe might sing.

The band begins to play an almost reggae or ska sort of beat. I can't help it and start to move to the music. Gabe clears his throat and calls crisply in an almost mourning tone.

"Roooooooxanne . . . you don't have to put on the red light. Those days are over. You don't have to sell your body to the night."

This song is amazing. Blake is grinning ear to ear and bobbing his head to the music. Abby and I move closer to the boys and compliment Blake on his find. Jay obviously loves it and dances from foot to foot in some sort of strange Irish, or maybe English, jig. Everyone gives the band their complete attention while swaying to the funky beat of the song. When the song is over, the entire party claps loudly, and the band takes a bow.

Gabe calls from the microphone. "We'll close this first set with a special guest."

There are murmurs running through the crowd followed by laughter, oohs and aahs as my uncle appears dressed in full Elvis attire. He is wearing a black wig and a sequined white jumpsuit with a cape. He steps up to the small stage and takes the microphone from Gabe.

"Thank you. Thank you very much." Uncle Ty says in a deep Elvis voice.

The crowd cheers and calls out song requests. So, Uncle Ty begins.

"Well, it's one for the money, two for the show, three to get ready, now go, go, go . . . but you, don't step on my blue suede shoes."

He is really good and sounds amazingly like Elvis. He continues to sing many great Elvis tunes, and the crowd can't get enough. He's sweating, and we are sweating from dancing and singing along in the heat of the Carolina night.

Uncle Ty closes with "Love Me Tender." It is so sweet. Abby and I watch him sing the entire song while staring right at Aunt Katy holding

Ben in her arms. I am embarrassed to say that I look over at Blake while the song is playing. I look straight into those turquoise blue eyes for a moment. We smile at one another and look away.

The band announces that it is time for them to eat, and they leave the stage. Fret, David and Blake come over to where Abby and I are standing by the edge of the pool. It is still a hot and humid evening even though it's approaching eleven. Lydia tells us from the shadows of the veranda that Uncle Ty will run us home as soon as he changes clothes.

"No time like the present then," says Fret.

"On three," yells David. "One, two, three!"

The boys come up behind me and Abby and shove us into the pool, clothes and all.

"I will get y'all for this!!!" shouts Abby.

The pool water is warm and refreshing.

"C'mon in. The water is great!" I splash and shout to no one and anyone in particular.

"Don't have to tell me twice," says Blake as he jumps in.

"Cannonball!!!" yells Fret, leaping from the diving board.

David follows right behind him and barely misses him in the water. Hank, Jay and Whitey are next followed by more kids and Ms. Claudette and Coach Clay. They giggle like children. Deena smiles while watching from the veranda with her parents, Granddad, Lydia and Ms. Hat.

I dive underwater and swim with my eyes open thinking about how lucky a kid must be to be a Feegan. To have two fun and loving parents, live in this great place and be talented too! They seem like the perfect family. I'm not jealous of that thought, only amazed.

Chapter 33

From the choir section at the front of the church, I have a clear view of my brothers. Neither one looks happy to be here this morning. I'm sure they are thinking of the fish they could be catching, or the pranks they could be pulling. Fret sees me looking at them and smiles. Jay continues to stare at the floor.

Lydia sits beside them on Fret's side looking like some sort of modern day American queen. She adores her costume jewelry. This morning, large cut crystal earrings dangle almost halfway to her shoulder. They match the brooch on her lapel. Lydia's reddish, strawberry-blond hair is always swept up in a French chignon, so earrings are an important part of her wardrobe.

I've only seen Lydia's hair down a couple times. One time was the middle of the night when we both went to check on a feverish Fret. The other time, she was in the laundry room coloring her hair in the big washtub. Both incidents were a bit frightening. She just didn't look like herself. This must have shown all over my face because Lydia laughed. She told me, *Beauty doesn't come easy at my age, Sug.*

Granddad sits on the other side of Jay with his eyes closed. Maybe he's praying, or napping, or thinking about fishing too. I feel a pang of guilt for taking all these boys out of their Sunday morning element with my singing.

This church is not large and can heat up very quickly after the people are all packed in tight. Mrs. Doyle takes a seat at the piano and nods to Father McClanagh as he passes on his way to the back of the church. I am sitting in the middle of the alto section. Abby smiles at me from her spot in front of the sopranos. The men stand in a single row behind the women of the choir.

Father McClanagh stands in the back at the end of the aisle with the altar servers, waiting for his cue. Abby stands and confidently moves to the microphone and lowers it to her level. Mrs. Doyle plays one lone note. Abby begins singing clearly, alone, a cappella.

"I the Lord of sea and sky. I have heard my people cry. All who dwell in dark and sin, my hand will save. I who made the stars of night. I will make their darkness bright. Who will be my light to them? Whom shall I send?"

The altar boy lifts the large wooden cross up in front of his face and begins walking. The other servers and Father follow him down the aisle.

The rest of the choir and Mrs. Doyle join Abby for the chorus.

"Here I am, Lord. Is it I, Lord? I have heard you calling in the night. I will go, Lord, if you lead me. I will hold your people in my heart."

The congregation is standing and singing loudly with emotion. I said it before, but it can be repeated. The Holy Spirit lives in this place. As the chorus comes to a close, I move forward to join Abby at the mike. Her momma smiles warmly at me and gives a nod of encouragement. I wasn't born to do this like Abby. I can't bear to look out at the congregation. My palms and armpits are sweating like crazy. I think I can even feel a drop of nervous sweat rolling down my back. I begin the verse with Abby.

"I the Lord of snow and rain. (Slowly) I have borne my people's pain. (Now building- I can hear Mrs. Doyle saying it in rehearsal.) I have wept for love of them. (With feeling) They turn away."

I realize Abby and I are harmonizing really well. I take a glance at the folks gathered here. I see smiles and tears of joy on the sea of faces. This encourages me to finish strong.

"I will break their hearts of stone, give them hearts for love alone. Who will speak my word to them? Whom shall I send?"

Abby squeezes my hand, but I let go quickly. I'm embarrassed by my sweating palm.

The entire place sings the chorus and the last verse enthusiastically. This song kills me every time. I typically lose it emotionally, and today is no different. Lydia is gazing in my direction. We wipe tears from our eyes at the exact same time. Some black ladies in the middle of the church are praising and singing with arms lifted and hips swaying.

Mrs. Doyle has just gone to town on the piano and is finishing with a flourish. We all sit down and wait for Father to begin the mass. I watch my brothers throughout the service. Fret occasionally fidgets in his seat. He gives me a smile and a thumbs-up sign every so often. Jay looks like he'd like to be anywhere but here. Granddad winks at me on occasion.

During his homily, Father McClanagh reads from the book of the prophet Isaiah. His faint Irish brogue makes the reading sound truly poetic, perhaps the way it is supposed to be read.

"Just as from the heavens the rain and snow come down
And do not return there til they have wetted the earth
Making it fertile and fruitful.
Giving seed to the one who sows, and bread to the one who eats.
So shall my word be- that goes forth from my mouth.
My word shall not return to me void
But shall do my will . . . achieving the end for which I send it.

"I happen to love this passage from Isaiah because it reminds me so of me homeland of Ireland. I picture our fertile hills and green valleys, our glorious countryside. Or picture the ebb and flow of your Low country tide in these fabulous rivers . . . a thunderstorm moving in late of an afternoon. This provides sustenance for the earth.

"Picture that rain as God's word pouring down. Did you feel the words of the opening hymn washing over you? I know I felt it. Thank you kindly, Mrs. Doyle."

He smiles in our direction.

"Let this provide you, along with the gift of the Eucharist. Let this provide each of you with the nourishment to be the hands of Christ for one another this week and always. Amen."

Chapter 34

I am again with Momma, this time in a small rowboat. We are together out on the river. I can hear the gulls squawking. Momma laughs. She has a beautiful, contagious laugh.

She is telling me a story from her own childhood spent on the river. She points out the old Guerreville site. She tells me that we will visit the site together one day. I try to tell her that Jay and I went there, but she doesn't seem to hear me.

I am so happy to be with Momma. Maybe I don't need to speak. I notice the freckles across the bridge of her nose and the way the sunlight makes her pale brown hair appear reddish. She wears a v-neck tee shirt, and I see that she still has the sunburn. I look down at her feet in the boat. She's wearing her favorite brown leather thong sandals. Her toenails are painted a pretty, pale pink. Typical of Momma, I think. Both Lydia and Grandma Rae wear red polish. Momma is pale pink. Gentle.

I smile and look in the direction of Guerreville where she's pointing. I look at her face and notice her smile fade as her hair darkens. The sunlight is caught up in a black cloud.

We both look to the southwest at the incoming clouds. A whip cracks in the direction of Guerreville. All I can think is that darn dream of mine is back.

There she is in all her glory. The Wicked Witch races along the river's edge in her black carriage. She cackles and points at me and Momma.

I lunge to grab hold of Momma. She is gone. As I reach for the nothing there, I find myself falling face-first into the dark river water.

Chapter 35

Well, that's some way to start a thirteenth birthday. Momma seemed so real in the dream. My heart still beats fast in my chest.

Having a thirteenth birthday could be exciting, except that my birthday also signals the end of our time here at Lydia and Granddad's. Daddy will be here tomorrow. I think he's only staying a few days before we drive home.

Lydia has always made my birthday special for me. She takes me shopping along King Street in Charleston and treats me to a fancy lunch and an ice cream sundae. She knows I prefer that over cake. Usually Granddad chauffeurs us around Charleston, but today Ms. Hat and Marcy are coming along. Marcy will do the driving.

Fret and Jay are out front washing Lydia's car. They give it a final drying wipe as Ms. Hat and Marcy pull up to the house in Marcy's little Gremlin. Granddad and Lydia come out the back door to greet them.

"Well, ladies, I'm not sure I appreciate being replaced like this." Granddad gives both Marcy and Ms. Hat hugs.

"Oh, Travis, you and the boys should be able to occupy your time just fine. I'm sure," Lydia says.

"What'll we do, boys?" Granddad asks. "Fishing then lunch out at Gracenote?"

"Sounds good to us, Granddad," Jay says, and Fret nods in agreement.

"Boys, that car looks divine. Why it's spotless!" Lydia exclaims.

"Maybe we should go into business, Jay," Fret says.

"The way you were waving that hose around, spraying me instead of the car. I don't think anyone would take us too seriously."

"Well, goodness gracious, what are we thinking? Happy Birthday, Sugar. I didn't even see you sitting there so quietly up on the veranda," Ms Hat calls.

Before lunch we stop in the Women's Crisis Center where Lydia, Ms. Hat and Marcy volunteer. The Crisis Center helps women in abusive relationships find safe places to stay, and they help pregnant women in need. The Center is located in a big, old boarding house in downtown Charleston. Each of the examination rooms and each apartment in the building is named for a donor who helped renovate the space. Today, the ladies want to show me a room that they worked to renovate and name in Momma's memory.

The Holy Spirit Church community helped put this together. The room will house an expectant mother and even her baby after it's born, if need be. It is beautiful to see. The walls are painted Momma's favorite robin's egg blue with a lovely toile fabric on the curtains and bedspread to match. Momma loved daisies too, so there are fresh daisies placed in vases around the little room. A placard on the door reads "Meredith's Room". Lydia hopes I can come back in the fall to meet the girl who will live here.

Mrs. Manier, the center's director, peeks into the room from the hallway.

"Happy Birthday, Emma."

I sit on the little bed with tears in my eyes. I wipe at my face with a tissue from the bedside table.

"I'm sorry," I begin. "I know my mom would have loved this very much."

"Of course she would have, dear," Mrs. Manier says. "Your momma volunteered here as soon as she learned how to drive. It was very important to her. I am pleased her memory lives on in this room. This will provide a safe haven for many young ladies in need of our help."

"Thank you, ma'am."

"You come back and visit us anytime, Emma. You are always welcome."

We are worn out from walking the streets of Charleston all morning by the time we sit down for lunch at Hardin's. Lydia greets the owners the same way she's been greeting folk all morning long up and down King Street, like she's known them all her life.

Marcy chats with our waitress as she leads us to a quiet spot in a back room on the second floor. Ms. Hat has lost a bit of her hearing, so she nods and smiles quite a bit when she isn't sure what's being said.

Hardin's restaurant faces one of the busier streets in Charleston. This is where we always come for my birthday lunch. I mean no offense to any of the ladies with me, but the hush puppies and shrimp and grits served here are to die for! Some folks get carried away putting a lot of cheddar cheese in their grits, but here the shrimp are doused in a delicious red-eye gravy. Not a lick of cheese in sight.

We snack on hush puppies and sweet tea while waiting for our meals to arrive.

"I can't believe Jack will be back tomorrow. Time flies," Marcy says.

"How long will he stay, Lydia, before the children have to leave?" Ms. Hat asks.

"I imagine they'll leave Saturday morning. Right, Sugar?"

"Probably. Daddy likes to get home in time to rest up a bit before the work week. Plus, Jay starts high school soccer practice next week."

Loud voices can be heard moving in our direction from somewhere in the restaurant. We don't think much of it until Marcy comments from her seat facing the door.

"Well, I'll be damned. Look what the cat drug in."

Chapter 36

H ello, Darlings."
We all turn to the door at once.

She kisses the hostess who led her back to us on both cheeks as if she's in France. She then turns in our direction and strikes a pose. One hand holds a long, thin cigarette in the air next to her face. The other hand rests lightly on her hip. Now that the hostess has gone, she isn't smiling.

Her dark hair is cropped short emphasizing her equally dark eyes. She wears tall black boots with stiletto heels, a dark gray knee-length, bias-cut skirt and a short black fitted jacket. A ruby red scarf completes her fashionable ensemble.

From what I can tell, my grandmother Rae Ann has always known how to make an entrance.

"Do you really think I was going to miss my only granddaughter's thirteenth birthday?"

"Hello, beautiful ladies. Let me drop these packages, and I'll be out of your hair."

Grandpa Tony brushes past his wife, smiling and moving in my direction.

"What on earth are y'all doing here?" Lydia asks.

"I have business in Charleston today. Rae Ann thought she'd make the drive in with me to join the celebration."

He winks at the other ladies while wrapping me in a giant bear hug.

Grandpa Tony is supposedly Grandma Rae's fifth husband. If that's the case, I'd say she finally got it right. I adore Grandpa Tony. He is small in stature, but his kind heart and warm smile are huge. He is neatly dressed (as always) in a light brown summer weight business suit with a French blue button down and a blue and gold paisley tie. He is originally from Chicago. Most of his large Italian family still lives there. He practices law in Greenville, South Carolina and lives there with Grandma Rae.

"I'll be back for you in a couple hours, dear. You ladies behave yourselves. Happy birthday, Emma. You are gorgeous. Thirteen, really? I hope you enjoy your gifts."

He kisses me on the cheek before leaving. Grandpa Tony never had children of his own, so he's pretty sweet about doting on me and my brothers along with his hordes of nieces and nephews back in Chicago.

"Well then . . . have a seat, Rae," Lydia says distractedly.

Grandma Rae kisses me on both cheeks with tears splashing from her eyes. I can smell smoke and alcohol on her breath. She greets Marcy, Lydia and Ms. Hat in the same fashion.

"Where did that darling waitress get to?" she asks.

"Here she is," Marcy says. "Tilly, could you please get Rae Ann a drink?"

"Darlin,' I'll have a vodka and water on ice with a lime."

"A vodka tonic?" Tilly asks.

"No, darling. Exactly what I said. Vodka, water, ice and lime. Heavier on vodka than water. Tell Larry it's for Rae Ann. He'll make it just right." She turns to the rest of us. "My doctor has prescribed this drink as a curative."

"A sort of hair of the dog that bit ya?" Lydia says with a chuckle to herself.

"Damn funny, Mother."

The waitress hesitates, looking uncomfortable, but states that she'll be back with more sweet tea for the rest of us.

"Oh, please don't tell me that I'm out to lunch with another boring bunch of broads. This seems to be the story of my life lately," Grandma Rae states flatly.

"Well, it isn't quite noon yet, Rae, and we are celebrating a child's birthday," Lydia says.

"Hell, I think I was already sneaking off to dance, drink and smoke out at Folly when I was damn close to thirteen," Grandma Rae replies.

"Please, Rae. You did some sneaking around from my recollection, but you wasn't thirteen when you did it," Ms. Hat chimes in.

"Had to drum up something to do being raised in that miserable little island community."

"I'd love to be raised there," I say.

"Well ain't you just a peach? Little gal created in Mother's own image," Grandma Rae nods in Lydia's direction as she says this.

"It's lovely that you decided to make the drive in with Tony today," Lydia says while attempting to change the subject.

"Mm-hmm. I do long to see Katy, Ty, Ben and the boys, but I don't think Tony can take the time. He's very busy with important mergers and acquisitions. If I have to host one more dinner party this month, I might throw myself off the Cooper River Bridge out there."

"Well, let's not do that," Marcy says.

"It's a joke really, Marc. I guess it does keep me occupied. That way I don't have time to think about the terrible loss I've suffered, once again."

She finishes her drink, lights a cigarette and signals the waitress with her empty glass.

"We've all suffered, haven't we, Rae?" Lydia asks.

Ms. Hat squeezes my hand beneath the table. I squeeze right back.

Our meals arrive, and the conversation quiets as we begin to eat. The shrimp and grits are delicious, but my appetite isn't what it was before Grandma Rae's arrival.

"Your father will be here tomorrow, Emma? A stop in Greenville on the way down would have been hospitable," Grandma Rae says between tiny bites of shrimp salad.

"That's right. I guess he'll stay for a few days before we go home," I tell her.

"Well, I've been on Tony to look into something for me," she begins as her words run together. "I don't know how one working man can raise three children alone. We have great schools in Greenville. Perhaps, my biological grandchildren could come stay with us."

"Oh, you've got to be kidding me. You couldn't even raise your own children. Besides, Jack has his own family close by in Indiana. I'm sure they'll help as much as he needs," Lydia says.

I'm watching Lydia's face. She, Marcy and Ms. Hat all looked shocked by what Grandma Rae has just suggested.

"It's not my business, Rae, but I think Jack is a fine father. He'll work things out for the kids," Marcy says.

Lydia interrupts. "Your biological grandchildren? Where does that leave Fret?"

"How dare you suggest that I couldn't raise my own children when you took them from me!" Grandma Rae turns on Lydia. "Biological because we look alike . . . folks might talk up in Greenville if Fret . . . You took my children from me. You ruined my life."

"Oh do you really want to go into why I took them from you? Is that a place you'd like to revisit, Rae Ann? Finding my granddaughter left in the hands, literally, of that raping, incestuous drunk that you called a husband. Was that husband two or three? The courts had no problem granting custody to me after that incident."

"Tilly, where is my drink? I need a damn drink!" Grandma Rae calls to the waitress.

"Ladies, it's Emma's birthday. Let's not fight," Marcy says.

"Rae, you was just too comely and inviting for your own good. That's what got you in trouble to start. All them boys coming around all the time. If you'd have paid attention to your school books rather than all that dancing, drinking and boy-chasing, things would have been just fine," Ms. Hat declares.

"You know your beloved Lydia killed my father and my Samson, Emma? Did you hear that story?" Rae asks meanly.

"As a matter of fact I did, ma'am. Lydia didn't kill them, Grandma Rae. They drowned." I'm certainly glad I know the story.

"Oh, she's a bossy woman, my mother," Rae begins. "She made Daddy go out in that river. She was always teasing him about his manhood. He had to prove himself once again. Well, I guess she got hers. He died. I guess I got mine too since my dear Samson and Daddy died."

"Rae, let's not talk about this now." Lydia tries to comfort her. "Not on Emma's birthday, please."

"Dammit. Now my Meredith is gone. Why is my life ruined again? What did I ever do to deserve all of this?"

Grandma Rae appears much more angry than sad. Ms. Hat squeezes my hand again. I am mad. I can't squeeze back.

"Maybe Momma is in a better place. That's what I have to believe. She was sad. Do any of you know that? Sure she was beautiful and gentle and could give that smile . . . She was charming, but often she was sad. Maybe you ruined her life, Grandma Rae. Did you ever think of that? She was hardly ever around anymore. She and Daddy fought all the time. I don't know where she was half the time. She wasn't home. You abandoned her, and now she's abandoned us. She didn't mean to, but it started even before she died. She tried not to do it. I know she tried. She and Daddy were getting along better right before. We all went to Disney and had the best vacation. But she still abandoned me. She still abandoned us."

My head is throbbing even though the tears won't come. I keep my chin tucked down. I look up to see that all the ladies are crying, even Grandma Rae. She gets up and leaves the room. Lydia comes over and pulls me close. Still I don't cry.

"Sug, it's okay. Sometimes you need to just let it out."

Ms. Hat rubs my back while muttering, "God bless you, Sugar."

Chapter 37

Grandma Rae didn't come back to the table after my outburst. She left in the same hasty fashion in which she appeared. I heard Lydia speaking to Grandpa Tony on the phone late last evening. From what I could tell, it sounded like he was apologizing. I heard Lydia tell him that she didn't need an apology from him. She told him that Grandma Rae should be apologizing to me.

That is just the problem with people like Rae. I know, Tony. Always the victim. She does not look at her own actions, ever. . . . To see how she might be treating people. I know I've dealt with it her whole life. Every damn thing is a personal affront. Yes, but this is Emma we're talking about here. A child. She can't even apologize to a child?

I crouched in the upstairs hallway listening to every word. She ended the conversation by telling Grandpa Tony to tell Grandma Rae that she owes me an apology. Somehow I doubt that message was passed along. It was given to a deaf ear anyway.

I've been helping Lydia or Granddad in the garden for the past few weeks before the activity of the day begins. I enjoy pulling weeds and pruning the plants. My brothers help mow the lawn, trim trees and bushes and help Granddad with other projects around the house.

I'm pulling weeds around the tomato plants when Lydia joins me. She doesn't look happy.

"You alright, Lydia?"

Kona drops a tennis ball right in front of me. I pick it up and throw it as far as I can towards the soccer goal.

"Just battling a mighty headache this morning, Sug. I should crawl back into bed, but I wanted to talk to you first. Could be the weather, I suppose, bringing this on. We're supposed to have quite a line of thunderstorms move through today. Hopefully your daddy makes it in ahead of them."

She's looking closely at a tomato plant as she talks. She pinches a large green worm off one of the vines. I don't know how she saw it. It looked like part of the plant to me. She squeezes the thing in two, drops it in the dirt, and wipes her hands on her black shorts.

"That's disgusting."

"Watch for worms masquerading as vines, Sug. They'll eat all the best that plant has to offer every time. We can't have them ruining our tomato crop."

Thunder rumbles in the distance.

"Lydia, I'm so sorry for the way I acted yesterday."

"Don't you worry your precious head, Sug. I'm sorry you were witness to such ugliness on your birthday of all days. Jesus help me."

We work on in silence. I gag whenever I come across a green worm, but I pinch the head off and throw it in the dirt. Just like Lydia showed me.

"It sounds like your momma may have suffered a sadness more than she ever told me, Emma."

"I'm sorry, Lydia. I shouldn't have talked about it."

"No. You should talk about it. Secrets fester. That could have been part of the problem."

"Did something happen to Momma?"

"She wasn't much older than you are now, Sug. I could kick myself and then some for coming home late on that day . . . for leaving her alone with Rae and that damn fool creep.

"Your momma was so sweet and gentle and innocent. She never would have provoked such behavior from a man, but this one was pure evil. His family was local, south Edisto way, but I haven't muttered their family name since that day. It doesn't bear repeating. To name him is to acknowledge his existence, and I'd rather not.

"Travis and I made a delivery into Charleston that morning. Thank God for Travis because if he hadn't been there, I'd be in prison to this day for cold-blooded murder. We loitered a bit in town chatting with friends. Rae had been home visiting us for a few weeks by that time. She and her husband of the moment. She was Ty and Meredith's mother after all. I thought it would be okay to leave them together for a short time. Meredith had taken to watching Ty when we had to run errands anyway.

"Travis and I arrived back at River Road to find Ty playing in the dirt and crying. He was about eight years old at the time. We asked him where Meredith was, and he pointed up River Road in the direction from which we had come. I asked him where his mother was, and he pointed to the house. He was crying a lot but not speaking at all.

"Travis stayed with Ty while I went into the house to find Rae. She was out on the sleeping porch, passed out. It looked like she and her lovely husband had shared a nice bottle of booze that morning in our absence. I shook her to try and wake her. I could have shaken that silly stupid woman to death. I was that frightened and angry.

Where is your damn fool of a husband? I screamed in her face.

What? I don't know. He wanted me to go to Guerreville this morning.

Guerreville? What on earth would he be doing out there? I yelled.

I dunno, Mother, for God's sake. Let me sleep.

"I pushed her down leaving bruises on her arms. I turned to see blood seeping down over her eyelid. She apparently hit her head on the table when I let go of her.

"I ran out to get Ty and Travis. Before getting in the car, I grabbed my rusty old paring knife from the garden. We got in and tore out of there for Guerreville. The old road back there was pretty well overgrown, but it was obvious that another car had come back through ahead of us. Fortunately, our neighbor, Gullekson, was part of our parish police patrol. We went flying by his house, stopping only long enough to tell him to follow us. He came as quick as he could.

"Ty sat in the back seat sobbing quietly. We parked behind that bastard's car. He must have been too drunk to hear us coming. Travis and I tore out of the car and took a run up the path. There he was. Our sweet Meredith was pinned beneath that monster.

"I could hear Travis and then Gullekson yelling after me. I was deaf and blind with rage. I held that knife in my hand. The first thing I did was run up on that poor excuse for a man and shove the knife right into his back. He screamed in agony, falling off of my dear Mere.

"Her eyes were glassy. She appeared to be in shock.

"Travis and Gullekson ripped him away from Mere. I kicked that disgusting excuse for a man so hard, he coughed up blood right then and there. I'd have finished killing him if I hadn't been in such a hurry to get to Mere.

"My Meredith. She was not responding at all. Gullekson told us to get her straight over to Dr. Kaseem. We did, and he helped her as best he could.

"Your momma was actually amazingly resilient, Sug. She was a little bit more withdrawn, but we all tried to be there for her. Your Grandma Rae, once again, blamed me for all of this. I pressed charges against her husband, so she left again. Because Officer Gullekson was witness to the entire event, Meredith didn't have to testify. That man was put away and didn't get out until shortly after she went away to college. I think that was another reason she chose to go so far away from home.

"Anyway, the real kicker came a couple months after the rape.

"Your momma seemed to be holding up pretty well, considering. Thank God for Travis and Ms. Hat's boys. Curtis and your momma were always close friends. She had Ty, and we were close to our priest at the time, Father John. He was a dear soul.

"She was fortunate to have Marcy as well. Marcy was actually the one who came to me. She told me that Mere thought she was pregnant. How I dreaded hearing those words.

"I went against all my Catholic schooling, all my best moral judgment. I went straight to Dr. Kaseem in my hatred and anger. I asked him to give Meredith an abortion.

"I'm sick even thinking about it right now.

"Of course it was illegal, but I was blinded by the disgust from the horrific act that caused this life to form. I refused to let that poor, innocent child bring a life into this world conceived in sin and evil.

"I put my friend, Dr. Kaseem, in a terrible quandary. He agreed to break the law and his own moral code as a physician to help Meredith. He tried to reason with me, but he wasn't very persuasive.

"I approached Meredith with my plan. God bless the sweet child. She was beside herself with guilt over the whole matter. She refused to terminate the pregnancy. She told me, *The Lord takes care of His own.* Just like that.

"*Lydia,* she said with a faraway look in her eyes, *the Lord takes care of His own.*

"I was sick with worry thinking her life was ruined. And that's how I found her under that old oak down by the river. She was bleeding something fierce. I couldn't help but think that the Lord really was taking care of His own.

"Later, she told me that she thought she was dying. If she was going to die, she wanted to die in her favorite spot on this earth. Under the tree and beside the river.

"She was pale as a ghost when I found her. I yelled to Granddad to run and fetch Dr. Kaseem. I wet my scarf in the river, held the child in my lap and let that cool water wash over her. All the time I prayed.

"It seemed we sat there for an eternity. She slipped in and out of consciousness, muttering about the embarrassment she had brought to the family.

"Dear Travis and Dr. Kaseem arrived and took the child off to the hospital in Charleston. She was weak with anemia from loss of blood. She had lost the baby, but she was going to be alright.

"I praised the Lord. In part, I thanked Him for taking that baby's life.

"Believe me, Sug. No matter how many times I'm reconciled with Jesus. I still cannot reconcile with myself. I think it's because part of asking forgiveness is truly feeling that what you've done is wrong. I come back to the thought often. If I were to do it all again, I would still want to kill that evil excuse for a man. It pains me to say it. Hell, I'm embarrassed to say it, but I still don't know how I would have felt if that baby had lived. I'm so sorry, Sug."

Chapter 38

L ydia went back to bed after our talk. I finish weeding the tomato bed with only my racing thoughts for company. Kona drops the tennis ball at my knees every so often. The sky is threatening a storm, definitely, but I'm going for a run.

I decide to run in the direction of Kiawah. Not too far though, just long enough to clear my thoughts a bit. Maybe I'll run out to the old Episcopal Church on Main Road and back. The clomping of my feet makes me feel awkward and heavy to start.

I feel bad for my outburst with Grandma Rae yesterday. I know I upset her, but what I really can't stand is the fact that I hurt Lydia. The road slopes from the middle down to the edge of the road to keep the rainwater from pooling. Every once in a while, sunlight filters through the oaks over my head, but mostly the dark clouds are moving in quickly.

The wind blows in my face. At least it will be at my back when I return. The distant sky is menacing. Lightning flashes. Thunder rumbles. Maybe I should turn back, but the run and the rain feel good. I can take cover at the church up on Main Road if necessary.

Momma and I ran to the church together last summer. We ran out and walked back to Lydia and Granddad's. She talked about being afraid of the little church when she was a kid. Now it has a fresh coat of white paint and a pretty picket fence surrounding its cemetery. She and Marcy always thought it was haunted. There's one small tomb there, and it was rumored that the girl laid to rest there was buried alive.

I turn onto Main Road now in the direction of the church. Wind whips the Spanish moss. The trees look creepy and alive. I think about turning around, but I'm closer to the church than anything else.

It seems as if someone has turned on the faucet full-throttle. The rain is driving hard into my face. Even on this warm summer morning, I feel chilled. My clothes stick to my skin, and my shoes slosh with each plodding step. I continue on to the church trying to run faster into the wind.

Last summer when we stopped at the church, Momma told me the story about the girl who was buried alive.

Her name was Eliza Grace Winsome, and she was visiting cousins out on one of the Kiawah plantations. There were only ever two there. She was a beautiful and charming young thing by all accounts. She became gravely ill while there on Kiawah. Many attempts were made to get her parents out to see her, but the tides and the weather would not cooperate. An early-season tropical storm had the water levels surging, and it was impossible for her father to navigate the treacherous waters from Charleston.

The doctor from Johns Island pronounced her dead before her parents could see her one last time.

In those days, folks were buried as soon as possible after death because there was no way to preserve the bodies. Little Eliza Grace was placed in the tomb outside the Episcopal Church. When her family finally made it out to the island from Charleston, they insisted that the tomb be opened. This was about a week after her burial.

The cemetery caretaker was shaking like the Spanish moss in a windstorm by the time this request was made. He was jumping at every little sound, each creak of a board in the old church, even a scampering mouse in the dead of night had him wide awake and quivering in his bed.

Why was that, Momma? I asked.

The first night after the girl was entombed the caretaker made his usual rounds. Locking the church up for the night. Blowing out the lanterns. He heard a whimpering sound. He thought perhaps an animal was hurt out in the cemetery. He tried to ignore it. The soft whimper continued. A scratching noise started in with the whimper. Mr. Leiner, the caretaker, decided to investigate. He unlocked the back door of the church and stepped out into the cemetery.

The night was black as ink. He walked over to where he thought the sound was coming from . . . over in the corner near the small tomb. He pressed his ear up next to the place where Eliza Grace Winsome's name was engraved. His heart beat rapidly inside his chest. All he could think was Edgar Allen Poe's poem about the telltale heart was coming to life. Suddenly, a piercing wail echoed in his ear. He fell over backwards trying to get away from the tomb.

As soon as he righted himself, he took off running into the darkness. He ran until he could run no more, and then walked back to the church. He told himself that it was just his imagination playing tricks on him. That night he wore his winter earmuffs to bed, just in case.

So, the girl's parents arrived and wanted him to open the tomb. Finally things had quieted, and he'd much rather let sleeping dogs lie. Of course he had no choice but to open the tomb. He reluctantly turned the key in the lock, and slid open the door.

The girl's mother saw the scene before them first and fainted dead away. Her father let out a blood-curdling scream. The caretaker's worst fears were realized.

The small casket had been pried open from the inside. The girl was lying in a heap on the floor of the tomb. Her hands and nails were caked with dried blood. The inside of the tomb door bore her scratch marks and her blood.

It has always been said that from that moment, the caretaker began a slow descent into madness. It was his job to make sure the tomb was locked. Interestingly enough, every lock he ever put on was mysteriously ripped off on the date of the girl's death every year.

A bolt of lightning cracks not too far away from me. I jump and run faster to the church. My shoes and socks are soaked and splattered with mud. I run around to the cemetery side of the church, open the gate, and slosh through soggy grass and mud to get to the church steps. A small overhang protects me from the weather.

Just then a brilliant flash lights up the sky. The tombstones are cast in an eerie glow for a moment. Now I understand why this place scared Momma as a child.

I move closer to the door of the church. The wind is blowing ferociously. Moss, twigs and leaves are flying across the cemetery lawn in the midst of a gloomy gray background. They catch on gravestones before coming to rest plastered up against the picket fence.

The sky is a strange yellow-gray like we see back home before a tornado. The earth trembles beneath my feet with each roll of thunder.

I'm soaking wet. I sit on my hands on the step trying to warm myself. Looking out over the gloomy landscape, I notice the small tomb in a back corner.

It reminds me of something Momma said last summer when she told me the story.

Em, the cemetery caretaker was forever haunted by the ghost of the little girl. Maybe because the girl's family never forgave him. They pretty much made his life hell after the opening of the tomb. He already blamed himself. Even though the doctor should have been at fault for declaring her dead, the family never granted Mr. Leiner the peace of their forgiveness. Maybe if the family had forgiven him, they all would have found some peace.

My lower back tightens as I lift myself from the hard church step. Walking into the wind and rain, I make my way out to the tomb.

Kneeling down in front of the pale ivory stone, I run my hand along the rough surface. The words are weather-worn. They are no longer readable. It looks like a bouquet of flowers was etched in the stone above the name and date.

I lay my forehead against the cool surface as a tear rolls down my cheek. Is the story true? I wonder.

Lydia talked the other day about the girl who killed Momma. She said it was a high school girl driving drunk. What kind of hell does she live in right now? Does Momma haunt her?

Chapter 39

E mma! Emma! My God, girl, what are you doing?"
  "Daddy?"
The van lights shine across the gravestones. Daddy looks scared to death as he jumps the fence and runs in my direction.

I'm faster than he is, jumping uneven headstones like some morbid Olympic hurdler trying to get to him.

"Dad!"

"Emma!"

He picks me up and practically squeezes the life out of me as we laugh and cry together.

"What the heck are you doing out here, Emma? Lydia has worried herself sick. I've been driving up and down these damn roads looking for you."

"I was here on the steps waiting out the storm. I'm fine."

"C'mon then . . . let's get back so she can have some peace of mind."

We climb up into the van. Dad smiles over at me and wipes a wet strand of hair out of my face. I notice that he appears youthful. He looks tan, thinner in a fit sort of way and well rested. His hair is cut shorter. He's not wearing his wedding band.

"I bought the Corvette, Em. You're going to love it."

"That's cool."

As we drive through the now ceasing storm back to Lydia and Granddad's, I want to ask Dad the questions. Does he miss Momma? Does he wonder about the girl who killed her? Does he forgive her?

But I don't ask. I know Dad doesn't like to talk about any of it. Sometimes I think he's madder at Momma herself than anything. I keep my mouth shut. I smile over at him as if everything is okay. Like always.

Chapter 40

The rain is falling softly and the sky is lightening. We pull into the River Road home. Jay and Fret run out to the van from the veranda. Kona is right behind them.

"Dad, Lydia's tree came down out front." Jay is out of breath. "I've never seen Lydia like this. Fretty and I both saw it. A bolt of lightning came out of nowhere and split the old oak in two!"

"Lydia's beside herself, Dad," Fret adds.

We circle around to the front where Granddad and Lydia are staring at the destruction. Lydia mumbles to herself. Her strawberry blond hair has fallen out of its typically neat chignon and swirls around her face.

The tree has fallen across the yard and the pier. The once-shady yard, perfectly enjoyable on a hot Low country afternoon, now seems exposed and naked.

Lydia doesn't even notice us. She sits right down in the muddy yard with her head cradled in her arms. Her hair drips with rain around her neck.

We stare silently. Fret goes over first and works his way onto Lydia's lap. She holds the gangly boy close resting her cheek on top of his head. Jay plops down on one side of her, so I take the other. Daddy sits next to Jay. Granddad paces back and forth in the wet grass.

Lydia notices my presence.

"Sugar, I was worried sick about you." She is crying.

"I'm fine, Lydia, just fine." Although the heat feels overwhelming right now in my damp clothing, and my head is pounding. I keep those thoughts to myself.

Because Lydia is crying, I suppose, Fret and I cry too.

"I'm sorry about your tree." Fret says.

"Oh, it's just a damn tree. But it sure has seen me through a lot," she says.

Granddad gently touches the top of my head and reaches out to Dad.

"You give me a hand, Jack?" he asks.

"Sure, Travis."

They return from the garden shed with chainsaws.

"I'm sorry, darling. We really need to get the pier cleared," Granddad says to Lydia.

"I know, sweetheart, but I can't bear to watch. Let's go inside, kids. It's stupid to be so upset. It's just a tree."

Kona chases after a small lizard under the fallen tree as we head into the house. My brothers and I sit on the banquette around the kitchen table.

"I used to spend hours watching your momma and Ty play under that tree." She smiles but tears glisten in the corners of her eyes. "Mere had a small wooden chest full of miniature dishes for tea. How she loved that thing. She'd lay a blanket down on the ground beneath the tree and play for hours. She had such a lovely imagination. I can still see the tiny little gal dressed in her Sunday best setting out tea service as if the Queen of England were joining her for crumpets. Why each of you has enjoyed climbing up in that tree."

Lydia angrily wipes at the tears on her face. I swear she looks like she's aged ten years today. She must have been in the middle of making her coffee when the storm hit. I get up and begin filling the percolator with cold water from the tap. Just like I've always seen Lydia do it, I measure four generous scoops of coffee from the tin into the filter basket.

Lydia turns to see what I'm doing, surprised.

"Well, I'll be . . . you making coffee, Sug?"

"Long as you don't mind it strong enough to bear up a horseshoe," I say while practicing my "Go to heck" eyebrow in the direction of the boys.

She laughs out loud. "Apple doesn't fall too far, I guess."

Chapter 41

We gather on the beach for our last night in the Low country. The bonfire burns bright and hot on this already warm night. It does keep the bugs away though.

Marcy and Curtis hold hands and smile at one another. They shared good news earlier in the day. They are expecting their first child shortly after Christmas. Ms. Hat sits between them and Lydia and Granddad looking pleased as punch with the news.

Dad, Fret and Jay are still splashing in the water with Ben and Aunt Katy watching from the shallows. Uncle Ty brings one last wagon full of picnic items down from the beach house.

I look down the beach and notice Abby, Blake, Hank and Whitey walking in our direction. David runs along ahead of them chasing seagulls. Kona takes off down the beach to greet them, and I run right behind her.

"We know it's a family gathering, Em, but we had to see you on your last night here."

Abby runs forward to give me a hug. Blake stops to play with Kona while watching me and Abby embrace. I feel like I'm going to cry, so I let go of my friend quickly.

Kona notices the Frisbee in Blake's hand. She's going crazy jumping at it and barking. Blake smiles and sends the Frisbee sailing perfectly down the beach into the wind. Kona sprints after it. She times her leap perfectly to catch the Frisbee square in her mouth as it's coming down.

"Man, I'd love to have a sporty dog like this. She is the coolest dog ever."

Blake pats Kona's head and takes the Frisbee from her mouth.

"Y'all still swimming?" Whitey yells out to Dad, Fret and Jay. "Don't those idiots know that sharks feed at dusk?"

He grins.

"Last one in's a rotten egg!"

The boys take off in the direction of the surf shedding shirts and flip-flops as they go.

* * *

It's getting late. I'm stuffed from eating boiled shrimp, pulled pork, cole slaw, and way too many hush puppies. Lydia made sangria for the adults. She knows how Dad loves her sangria.

The boys have wandered down the beach looking for nesting sea turtles. Curtis reminded them to turn off their flashlights if they see one.

Abby's momma picked her up a short while ago.

I curl up in a lounge chair near the fire and wrap myself in a blanket. Kona seems to sense my sadness. Normally she'd be off chasing after the boys. Tonight she curls up next to my chair in the sand. She paws at the occasional ghost crab scampering by. I lay on my side looking out to sea. Clouds pass over the moon, but the reflection is beautiful each time they clear. The wind blows through my hair. I'm comforted by this, as if God were caressing my cheek.

"Just can't get over how bare the front yard looks without the oak."

Lydia's gravelly voice breaks the silence of my thoughts.

"We'll plant a new one in the same spot. Lydia. I promise," Uncle Ty says.

"All well and good, dear. I fear I won't even live to see it provide shade to a grasshopper."

"Lydia! That's nonsense," Ms. Hat tells her.

"Oh, you know what I mean, Hat."

"I remember the first time I came down to meet you all."

This is Dad speaking. I can hardly believe it. He's not the sharing type. I wonder how much of that sangria he's had.

He continues, "Mere couldn't wait to show me the River Road home, the river and the huge oak. She told me stories about how she climbed it and played beneath it as a child. Naturally, I was drawn to the river when I first went around the house. I started for the pier, but she grabbed my hand and ran me right over to the tree."

I can hear the smile and the love in his voice.

"She climbed right up there as if she was still a small child. She encouraged me to follow. As soon as we got up in there, I understood. There was sort of a human sized nest up there. The branches came together perfectly for two people to comfortably sit."

"Oh, Lordy. Mere and I spent so much time up in that old tree," Marcy adds. "We used to spy on the adults on the veranda. Half the time they didn't even know we were there." She giggles.

"Yes. We could see the veranda through the leaves, but the view of the river blew me away. It was the most beautiful sight I'd ever seen. I remember clearly how Meredith pointed out the marsh grass blowing in the breeze. We saw a pod of dolphins swimming gently along and watched pelicans diving into the water after fish.

"To see the joy on her face as she shared this scene, this place with me. I was overcome with emotion. In my mind I vowed right then and there that I would love this beautiful brown-eyed girl forever. I wanted to take her in my arms and never let her go."

I can hear the sadness creep into Dad's voice, but I don't turn away from the water to look at him. His voice cracks as he continues.

"I think it was very difficult for her to live away from this place and all of you. Maybe I should have paid closer attention to that."

"Jack, don't we all miss our childhood a bit when we're grown?" Lydia asks. "Sometimes we miss a moment in time more than a place."

"She sure brought great joy and laughter to this place," Granddad says.

"She was a joyful child," Ms. Hat says.

"She was always finding some critter needing care. Remember, Lydia?" Uncle Ty asks. "For awhile she took care of a baby egret. That thing would eat shrimp right out of her hand."

"Yes, Bongo was his name," says Marcy.

"Bongo! That's it."

Marcy and Uncle Ty laugh quietly.

"Well, that sure didn't stop up north. Do you know how many cats and dogs and bunnies have moved in and out of our home?" Dad asks.

"We have Meredith to thank for Kona. She was down visiting when the kids were younger, remember? The lady working at the post office in Charleston was giving those pups away. The momma was a Border collie and the daddy snuck in under the fence. Of course, Mere and the kids couldn't walk by without thinking that Travis and I needed a puppy. Well, she was right. Kona has been a Godsend."

I close my eyes and remember that day. I must have been five or six at the time. Kona and her little puppy siblings were the cutest things I had ever seen. I was so happy! Momma let me and Jay take turns holding her on the ride back to River Road. Fretty laughed and laughed every time Kona licked his face.

"Remember when y'all had that little sunfish sailboat?" Marcy asks. "Mere knew I was deathly afraid of snakes. We had a couple other girls with us. Claudette, I think. Well, a snake went swimming right by Mere. Swimming in the river! She grabbed that durned thing by the tail and flung it right up onto the boat! I screamed and fell out of the boat. Landed right next to the spot where that snake lit. He was more afraid of me and the noise I was making than I was of him, I guess. That thing took off faster than I could say 'boo!'"

"She used to laugh every time she told me that story, Marc," Dad says.

"She was a real sweetheart, a gem," says Ms. Hat.

"These kids are only going to become more busy, Jack," Lydia says after a brief silence.

"I know, Lydia."

"Please don't be strangers."

Chapter 42

I wait for Blake out in front of the beach house. And I wait.
Typical, I think. I take off walking down to the river by myself.
Maybe it's just as well. The tide should be pretty far out by the time I get there.

I breathe deeply and slowly trying to inject this thick, salty air into every fiber of my being. Leaving this place is never easy.

Looking out over the waves of the Atlantic, I notice pelicans bobbing in the breakers. The sight makes me smile.

A huge horseshoe crab is washed up on shore. Curtis once told us that they really aren't crabs at all. They're more closely related to spiders and scorpions. I flip the big guy over to see if he's still among the living.

His strange claw-like tentacles stretch toward my face.

"Ew!" I drop him back over quickly, and pick him up so that his tentacles are pointing at the sand. He's heavy. Holding him as far away from me as I can, I walk him down and place him knee deep in the surf.

The water is warm as it always seems to be on a sunny summer day. I stand still for a moment to let the gentle waves splash across my thighs. I rinse any horseshoe crab juice off my hands and continue down the beach.

It is still very early. The tide chart said low tide would be at 7:13 this morning. It looks like it must be close to that time as I approach the river.

The scene before me is one of my favorites. The waves are breaking far out into the water at the sandbar that almost bridges Kiawah to Seabrook Island to the southwest. The shallow waters shimmer between the beach and the sandbar. I run out into the shallows, giggling at the sight of blue crabs scattering every which way.

It's kind of a hydrangea blue morning sky reflected in the water. A blue crab skitters in my direction snapping his claws. I jump out of his way, and he shimmies right on by. Momma used to joke about these crabs. She said they must know how much I love crab cakes and she-crab soup because they seem to target me specifically.

Is this a glimpse of heaven? Lazy summer days, deep blue skies, miles of quiet beach, and the sound of waves gently folding onto the shore? Is Momma there standing with Jesus, smiling down and wishing us well?

Looking over to the river, I see a small group of people gathered on the Seabrook side. Some are on horseback, and they are pointing upstream. I know the dolphins must be there enjoying their breakfast.

I turn to walk upstream along the river, and there he is. He struggles on the steep bank to pull his little skiff up on shore.

Butterflies. Why does my stomach do that? He's wearing only swim trunks. I can't help but notice the muscles in his tanned back as he struggles with the boat.

"Blake, can I help you?"

"I've got it, Em. Thanks though."

I move next to him and grab a hold of the boat anyway. We both pull. Suddenly the boat lets loose of whatever it was stuck on. It breaks free, and we topple backwards in the process.

I practically land in Blake's lap. He holds onto me for the briefest of moments. His hands placed gently around my waist. A shiver runs down my spine. I turn to look at him. His gorgeous blue eyes are staring straight into mine.

We kiss.

What am I doing? I think I put my lips on his first! We're kissing. Okay. This is embarrassing. Well, this is nice. I feel his hand gently pressing the small of my back.

I push away awkwardly. The folks over on the Seabrook bank must be watching. Fortunately, it looks like the boat might block their view.

We both laugh self-consciously.

"Thanks, Emma. That was nice. I've wanted to kiss you since the day we met."

"Well, that would have been even more awkward," I say. "What happened to you? I thought you were going to meet me at the beach house."

"I got up late and thought the quickest way to find you would be in my boat. Are you really leaving today? You'll keep in touch, won't you?"

"We are leaving, and definitely we'll keep in touch."

"You want to go out on the river for a little ride in the skiff? See if we can find some more dolphins?"

"After all that work bringing your boat on shore?"

"I wouldn't mind doing all that again."

Maybe he notices my embarrassment. He picks me up and sets me in the skiff.

"Hey wait for me!"

Fret is riding his bike in our direction. His skinny legs are moving as fast as they can go.

"Daddy sent me down to check on you, Em."

Blake and I exchange a glance. I'm relieved Fret's here.

"C'mon, Fret. You wanna come on a short ride with us?" Blake asks.

He sounds relieved as well.

Chapter 43

I sit on the bed and stare absentmindedly at the fresh vase of hydrangeas. Lydia must have placed them there yesterday. My bags are packed, next to the door.

The dark purpley-blue color of the hydrangeas reminds me of lilacs in spring back home. I do look forward to seeing our family and my friends back in Indiana.

The cemetery where Momma's buried is just a few blocks from our house. In elementary school me, my brothers and our friends would hop the fence at the end of Crescent Street and shortcut through the cemetery to get to and from school.

Some folks might think cemeteries are morbid, but my friends and I think Rice Cemetery is a beautiful place. Lauren, Jess and I would often picnic there in the late spring and early summer. A lot of local history can be learned in a cemetery too. We'd wander around looking at the old tombstones. We'd marvel at the gigantic Greek-columned arbor that one of our town's early founders dedicated to his deceased wife and infant daughter.

Lauren and Jess weren't sure how I'd feel about a picnic in the cemetery after Momma was buried there. They invited me anyway.

It was just a few weeks after Momma died, and the headstone had just been placed. It read "Meredith R. Phend, wife and mother" with the dates. I remember seeing that and thinking I should have been in charge of what was written. There could be many more poetic ways of describing all that my sweet mother had been.

But as I sat there with my dear friends, eating peanut butter sandwiches and sipping lemonade, I thought "wife and mother" was perfectly simple and to the point.

Mere words can never capture exactly what it feels to lose someone you've loved. I suppose most people feel that way. It's more in mind-pictures we have of that person, snippets of conversation and smells. Yes, smells.

Momma loved lilacs. We lived in two different homes on our street. One was very traditional and the other, contemporary, but both backyards grew lilacs in abundance.

And that's when I realized the cemetery was still a peaceful and pretty place for me to visit. Especially with Momma being buried there.

Jess, Lauren and I ate our lunch, and I smelled the lilacs. Looking around at Momma's final resting place, I saw many of her favorite bushes tucked here and there. In that moment, she was alive and with me again. In the smell of the lilacs.

Lydia looks in on me from the hallway. She looks tired, older.

"I certainly don't want to rush you, Sug, but your daddy and the boys are waiting for you outside."

She comes and sits next to me on the big bed. She lets out a deep sigh.

"It has been an absolute joy having you here, Sugar. I simply abhor good byes. We'll just have to look forward to meeting again." She smiles and pats my knee. "You've gotten brown as a berry down here."

"I love you, Lydia. I'll miss you too. Thanks for everything." I grasp her hand in mine and hold it against my cheek for a moment.

"You call if you need anything, okay?" she says seriously. "And make sure you help your daddy around the house. I told the boys the same thing. And remember, the Lord helps those who help themselves. Do you know what that means?"

"Well, I kind of take it to mean that I shouldn't go around feeling sorry for myself because I lost my momma. I should carry on with my life?" I'm not sure what she's looking for here.

"In part, Sugar. You did lose your momma, darling. That gives you the right to have a good cry anytime you feel like it," she smiles in a sad way. "The Lord helps those who help themselves. That means be diligent in your prayer, Sug. Don't be afraid, ever, to ask the good Lord to be your guide, but here's the tricky part. You have to be smart enough to hear the answer. Most folks don't ever listen to what God is trying to tell them. They need to be hit upside the head to hear it. No, God speaks to us in many different ways. So, you have to be still enough and clever enough to hear the message. I know you are. Just don't forget it."

I hug Lydia and think about this.

Dad is calling me to hurry down and tell everyone good bye. I happen to hate good byes as well.

"Come on, Sug. We'd best be getting down there and seeing y'all off." Lydia likes to lay on the Southern accent a bit thicker when we're leaving town.

I slip my feet into my flip-flops, glance approvingly at my freshly painted pink toenails, grab my bags from the floor and trot behind Lydia down the mahogany-floored hallway to my waiting family.

"Oh, I forgot!"

I run back and open the large chest of drawers. I grab the old cross-shaped tool and tuck it securely into my pocket.

Chapter 44

S ometimes God speaks to me in the wee hours of the morning. I don't mean I hear a booming, out-loud voice like Moses might have heard. I simply wake with a thought that I know comes from the word of God.

I'm in my room in Indiana. Momma and I decorated this room together. It has a pretty yellow floral-print bedspread, yellow and white-striped curtains, and bookshelves completely covering one wall.

But my dream was set in the Low country.

I was standing alone in Lydia and Granddad's front yard. At least I thought I was alone.

Where the old live oak had fallen, there is a gaping hole in its place. The river churns angrily, and I see shark fins circling out in the water. There are a couple large alligators lying silently upon the river bank. A light-skinned black man sits in a john-boat out in the river beckoning for me to help him. Actually, he's calling "Rae Ann!" He apparently thinks that I am my grandmother. The sky is dark and threatening rain at any moment.

Suddenly, flowers start growing out of the hole where the tree once stood. They're growing fast and spreading across the yard. As they begin to surround the spot where I stand, I notice the man in the boat being pushed away in the water by an older man with gray hair. They both smile eerily in my direction as they leave. The waters become calm. The sharks and alligators are gone too. The sun comes out causing the river to turn a vibrant turquoise blue.

The blue of the river reminds me of Blake's eyes. Just as I have that thought, he and his sister, Deena, come walking around the house.

Blake is throwing a Frisbee to a very happy Kona as they walk. They wave but don't come over to speak to me.

Blake and Deena seem to walk on top of the flowers covering the lawn, almost gliding. Kona leaps through the blossoms like a deer. There is movement behind me, and Lydia and Granddad Travis appear on the veranda. Lydia stands looking out to the river. She is wearing a beautiful white dress with a red geranium print. It is fitted at the bodice and flares out at her waist stopping just below her knees. She wears red high-heeled peep-toe sandals. Of course her toenails are painted to match the outfit. Granddad is looking dapper on the veranda. He sits in khakis, black loafers, black belt and a white button-down. Normally, he might be smoking a cigarette, but instead he is chewing on the stem of a daisy and smiling in the direction of the river as well.

I follow their gaze. Blake and Deena are looking in the same direction. Uncle Ty, Aunt Katy and Ben are now sitting at the end of the pier. They look off into the distance up the river in the direction of the west end of Kiawah and Seabrook.

A great blue heron can be seen in the distance flying gracefully up the river. She glides in and lands on the end of the pier right next to Ben. No one seems alarmed by this, and Ben just laughs.

The heron turns her head toward Uncle Ty. He pulls a shrimp from a small bucket and feeds it to the gorgeous bird. Aunt Katy and Ben take turns petting her back. The bird seems to turn and stare ever so briefly and lovingly at Lydia, Granddad, Blake and Deena.

The bird takes flight from the end of the pier. She is flying straight at me and comes close enough that I am knocked over backwards. I feel afraid as I fall but land in a heap in the flowers. The smell of lilacs fills the air. As the heron passes over me, I am flooded with a feeling of sadness mixed with both gratitude and love.

The End

LaVergne, TN USA
04 November 2010

203588LV00001B/4/P